"Do you trust me after all?"

Jessica bit her lip, wondering how she was supposed to answer that. She didn't have to see Sam's face to know he was frowning. "If I didn't trust you, would I be sharing a hotel room with you?"

"That does take a certain leap of faith. But it isn't really what I asked you."

"You want to know if I still think you're trying to stop me from seeing my mother."

"Right."

The darkness made it easier for her to be honest. "I can't figure out why you would suddenly be on my side. I don't know what's in it for you."

"You think there has to be something in it for me?"

He sounded more curious than offended. "Yes," she said simply. "I just haven't figured out what it is yet."

Dear Reader,

It's hard to believe that it's *that* time of year again—and what better way to escape the holiday hysteria than with a good book…or six! Our selections begin with Allison Leigh's *The Truth About the Tycoon,* as a man bent on revenge finds his plans have hit a snag—in the form of the beautiful sister of the man he's out to get.

THE PARKS EMPIRE concludes its six-book run with *The Homecoming* by Gina Wilkins, in which Walter Parks's daughter tries to free her mother from the clutches of her unscrupulous father. Too bad the handsome detective working for her dad is hot on her trail! *The M.D.'s Surprise Family* by Marie Ferrarella is another in her popular miniseries THE BACHELORS OF BLAIR MEMORIAL. This time, a lonely woman looking for a doctor to save her little brother finds both a healer of bodies and of hearts in the handsome neurosurgeon who comes highly recommended. In *A Kiss in the Moonlight,* another in Laurie Paige's SEVEN DEVILS miniseries, a woman can't resist her attraction to the man she let get away—because guilt was pulling her in another direction. But now he's back in her sights—soon to be in her clutches? In Karen Rose Smith's *Which Child Is Mine?* a woman is torn between the child she gave birth to and the one she's been raising. And the only way out seems to be to marry the man who fathered her "daughter." Last, a man decides to reclaim everything he's always wanted, in the form of his biological daughters, and their mother, in Sharon De Vita's *Rightfully His.*

Here's hoping every one of your holiday wishes comes true, and we look forward to celebrating the New Year with you.

All the best,

Gail Chasan
Senior Editor

Please address questions and book requests to:
Silhouette Reader Service
U.S.: 3010 Walden Ave., P.O. Box 1325, Buffalo, NY 14269
Canadian: P.O. Box 609, Fort Erie, Ont. L2A 5X3

The Homecoming

GINA WILKINS

Silhouette

SPECIAL EDITION

Published by Silhouette Books

America's Publisher of Contemporary Romance

For my brother-in-law, Mike Wilkinson.
Thanks for the travel info! Any errors are all mine.

Special thanks and acknowledgment are given to
Gina Wilkins for her contribution to
THE PARKS EMPIRE series.

 SILHOUETTE BOOKS

ISBN 0-373-24652-8

THE HOMECOMING

Copyright © 2004 by Harlequin Books S.A.

Books by Gina Wilkins

Silhouette Special Edition

The Father Next Door #1082
It Could Happen To You #1119
Valentine Baby #1153
†*Her Very Own Family* #1243
†*That First Special Kiss* #1269
Surprise Partners #1318
**The Stranger in Room 205* #1399
**Bachelor Cop Finally
    Caught?* #1413
**Dateline Matrimony* #1424
The Groom's Stand-In #1460
The Best Man's Plan #1479
The Family Plan #1525
Conflict of Interest #1531
Faith, Hope and Family #1538
Make-Believe Mistletoe #1583
Countdown to Baby #1592
The Homecoming #1652

Silhouette Books

World's Most Eligible Bachelors
Doctor in Disguise

†Family Found: Sons & Daughters
**Hot Off the Press
§Family Found
‡The Family Way
*The McClouds of Mississippi

**Previously published
as Gina Ferris**

Silhouette Special Edition

Healing Sympathy #496
Lady Beware #549
In from the Rain #677
Prodigal Father #711
§*Full of Grace* #793
§*Hardworking Man* #806
§*Fair and Wise* #819
§*Far To Go* #862
§*Loving and Giving* #879
Babies on Board #913

**Previously published
as Gina Ferris Wilkins**

Silhouette Special Edition

‡*A Man for Mom* #955
‡*A Match for Celia* #967
‡*A Home for Adam* #980
‡*Cody's Fiancée* #1006

Silhouette Books

Mother's Day Collection 1995
Three Mothers and a Cradle
    "Beginnings"

GINA WILKINS

is a bestselling and award-winning author who has written more than sixty-five books for Harlequin and Silhouette. She credits her successful career in romance to her long, happy marriage and her three "extraordinary" children.

A lifelong resident of central Arkansas, Ms. Wilkins sold her first book to Harlequin in 1987 and has been writing full-time since. She has appeared on the Waldenbooks, B. Dalton and *USA TODAY* bestseller lists. She is a three-time recipient of the Maggie Award for Excellence, sponsored by Georgia Romance Writers, and has won several awards from the reviewers of *Romantic Times*.

THE PARKS EMPIRE

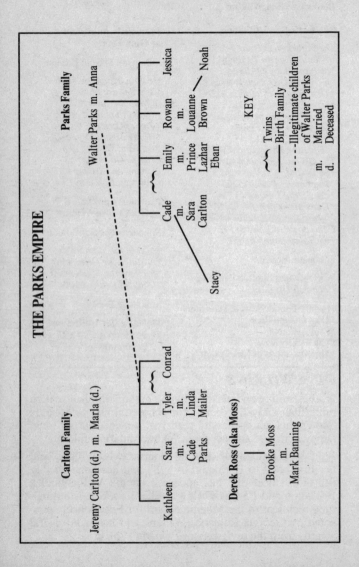

Carlton Family

Jeremy Carlton (d.) m. Marla (d.)

Kathleen

Sara
m.
Cade
Parks

Tyler
m.
Linda
Mailer

Conrad

Derek Ross (aka Moss)

Brooke Moss
m.
Mark Banning

Parks Family

Walter Parks m. Anna

Cade
m.
Sara
Carlton

Emily
m.
Prince
Lazhar
Eban

Rowan
m.
Louanne
Brown

Jessica

Noah

Stacy

KEY

⌣ Twins
— Birth Family
----- Illegitimate children
of Walter Parks
m. Married
d. Deceased

Prologue

The bracelet in Jessica Parks's hand was undeniably pretty. Multicolored semiprecious stones were set in sterling silver, their facets catching the light and cheerily scattering it. But looking at the lovely bauble brought her no pleasure at all. Instead, she was filled with consternation at having found it in the pocket of the long black sweater jacket she wore over a white T-shirt and snug black pants.

She didn't recall putting the bracelet in her pocket. She remembered admiring it at a department store she had visited with her best friend, Caroline, but she had no recollection of slipping it into her jacket.

Swallowing hard, she turned to open a center drawer in her cherry dresser. Inside the velvet-lined drawer rested five small, easily pocketed items—six, once she added this bracelet. Ranging from a pair of gold earrings to a little cloisonné box shaped like a grand piano, the baubles had all shown up in her possession during the past year. Sometimes she found them in her pocket, sometimes in her purse, and one—a miniature crystal rose—she had found hidden in an art portfolio she had carried with her on a shopping and sketching outing. Sometimes she had been alone on those outings, other times with Caroline, but she never remembered taking anything.

Stashing the bracelet among the other things, she closed the drawer quickly, as if not seeing the purloined items would make them disappear. She knew she should do something with them—specifically, try to figure out a way to return them to their stores—but she just couldn't deal with that task yet.

The unremembered shoplifting incidents—for want of a better term—were disturbing enough, considering that she'd had a little habit of taking things as an angry and rebellious teenager. But she had always remembered those events, had been very deliberate about what she had taken and why. Most of her petty larcenies in the past had been aimed at her father, either from the jewelry stores he owned or from his office or study—and usually intended to provide cash for things she wanted to do that he had forbidden. But this was very different.

There were other episodes. Finding her keys locked in her car when she had been certain she'd carried them inside. Finding her wallet in the freezer and a melted container of ice cream in her art studio. Discovering cosmetics she didn't remember buying stashed neatly inside her makeup case.

More disturbing, on three occasions finding odd additions made to paintings in progress in her studio. Undoubtedly her own style of painting—but additions she simply didn't remember making.

Definitely not normal behavior. And it seemed to be getting worse, especially during the last few weeks as she had dealt with the tension of making secret plans in addition to her powerful and controlling father's arrest.

She should tell someone what was going on—a medical professional, at least—but she refused to give anyone evidence that she was becoming emotionally unstable. Especially not now, when she was so close to seeing the culmination of a plan she had been carefully putting together for what seemed like most of her twenty-six years.

She could handle this, she assured herself. Whether her odd behavior was due to stress or anxiety or simply artistic absentmindedness, she would get control of it through the force of sheer willpower. Perhaps she had inherited some of her mother's emotional instability, but it was combined with a streak of her father's ruthless determination.

She wasn't letting anything—or any*one*—stand in her way this time.

Chapter One

Sam Fields waited until Jessica's little red sports car was well out of sight before he broke into her cottage.

There was no need to follow her this time; he knew where she was going. She spent every Wednesday afternoon as a volunteer art teacher at a San Francisco school for emotionally disturbed teenagers. If she followed her usual routine, she would be gone for three hours, after which she would return and retreat to her art studio until late into the night. Something about her volunteer work always seemed to spark her creativity.

Just for curiosity, he walked into her studio after letting himself into her tidy, eclectically decorated cottage. Though he had never been inside the cottage before, he had no trouble finding the studio. The cottage wasn't big enough to get lost in, unlike the mansion just next door in which she had grown up.

He spent quite a while—too long, perhaps—studying the paintings sitting on easels and stacked against the walls. He had seen her work before, in local galleries, and he was always taken aback by the sheer power of it. It surprised him that such a delicate, almost fragile-looking young woman could create such bold, intellectually challenging works of art.

Had he guessed at her work judging solely by her appearance—a petite, fair-skinned blonde whose dimpled oval face was dominated by astonishingly blue eyes—he would have expected pretty watercolors or tidy still-life studies. Instead, her paintings were unpredictable and untamed, with strong hints of rebellion, anger and simmering sensuality.

His attention was drawn to three canvases propped in a corner, backs facing the room. None of them were finished, he noted when he flipped through them. It was as if she had reached a certain point with each and had stopped. Perhaps she had been unhappy with the way they were turning out.

As he studied them more closely, he could see that they were different, somehow, from her other works. Similar enough that he recognized the style, but more disturbing in content. Some additions seemed to have been slapped on in periods of extreme emotion, and others looked almost assembly line, as if painted by a computerized robot. Paintings that seemed to have begun with one theme had been abruptly altered, then abandoned.

Odd, he thought, putting everything back exactly as

he had found it. But then, he had come to expect odd behavior from Jessica Parks.

Methodically searching the little cottage in which she lived on her father's impressive Pacific Heights estate, he found little of interest until he reached her bedroom. A hardcover romantic suspense novel lay facedown on the nightstand, a bookmark showing it to be half-read. No photographs were displayed in the room, framed or otherwise.

Ignoring the frilly garments that might have intrigued him had he allowed himself to picture her in them, he rummaged through the vanity and dresser drawers. No diary or stashed letters, the two specific items he had been instructed to search for as a clue to her recent behavior. She must keep things like that well hidden, somewhere that would take a bit more effort to find. He found nothing at all of note until he opened a small drawer in the center of her dresser.

He looked thoughtfully at the disparate stash of baubles lying on the velvet lining. All were obviously new, some still bearing price tags. Picking up the stone-and-silver bracelet, he let it dangle from his fingers for a few long moments, his lips pursed thoughtfully. And then he replaced it with the other items, exactly the way he had found it.

A short while later, with plenty of time to spare before Jessica returned, he let himself out of the house, making sure the door locked behind him.

Jessica was being followed. And it wasn't the first time. She even recognized the guy. He was the same one who had been tailing her on and off for a couple of months.

He was wearing one of his disguises again—this time a scruffy, dirty brown wig pulled into a ponytail beneath a black knit cap. A pair of oversize dark glasses covered most of his face. He wore a grubby denim jacket over an untucked flannel shirt and faded jeans. She recognized him, just as she had made him in a tailored business suit, motorcycle garb, even a city sanitation worker's uniform once.

There was something about the way he moved that made him stand out to her, even in a crowd. Apparently he hadn't taken into account that she was an artist with a keen eye for details.

She didn't like to think of the number of times he might have spied on her without her seeing him. And she didn't want to know what sort of impressions he had formed of her while watching her—impressions he would have dutifully reported to the man she was certain had hired him.

Because it made her so nervous, she always seemed to do something stupid when she spotted him. Like the time she had knocked over a display of art supplies, causing such a mess in her favorite art store that she had been too embarrassed to go back since. Another time, she had dashed out of a department store without realizing she was still holding a silk T-shirt she'd been admiring when she saw him. The resulting clamor of alarms at the door had been humiliating.

She had babbled some explanation to the employee at the door about feeling light-headed and needing fresh air, then had bought the expensive T-shirt in three different colors just to prove she had intended to buy it all along. That purchase had cleaned out her checking account, resulting in several weeks of scrimping before the sale of two paintings had replenished the finances her father controlled with such a tight fist.

She wouldn't do anything stupid this time, she promised herself with a deep, steadying breath, but she would give her unwelcome shadow the slip. He couldn't be allowed to spy on the secret meeting she was to attend in less than an hour.

Making sure there was nothing in her hands—or her pockets—she glanced furtively around the pharmacy she had popped into for a refill of the medicine she took for occasional migraines. The man was now skulking on the other side of the store, examining a rack of over-the-counter pain relievers.

Wishing she could personally give him a reason to need an analgesic, she slipped through a narrow row of feminine hygiene products, then dashed out a side door and into a long, dim alleyway. She hoped by the time the guy realized she was no longer in the feminine products aisle, she would be too far away for him to find her again.

It was a heavily overcast afternoon, typical for San Francisco in early November. Gray clouds continued to deepen, throwing the alley into shadows that made it look more like early evening than midafternoon. She never even saw a man standing in the darkness of a recessed doorway until he stepped out in front of her.

Stumbling to a stop, she pressed a hand against her pounding heart. Her first thought was that it was the man she had escaped in the pharmacy, that he had somehow gotten ahead of her. But a second look showed her that this was a stranger. A very large and mean-looking stranger.

The man who had been following her was perhaps six feet tall and slim—this guy was a six-foot-five mountain.

"Excuse me," she said, making an effort to keep her voice brusque and her manner confident. "You're blocking my way."

"Am I now?" His face looked strange in the shadows, filled with deep hollows and sharp angles. His dark eyes swept her body with an insolence that set her teeth on edge.

"Yes." She took a step sideways, hoping he would let her pass now that he'd had fun scaring the spit out of her.

He moved in front of her again, taking a step closer at the same time. "Don't be in such a hurry."

Abruptly deciding she would rather take her chances with the man who had been following her than with this guy, Jessica turned on one heel to dart back in the other direction. Moving with a speed she wouldn't have expected from someone so large, the man grabbed her from behind.

After being mugged by a purse snatcher five years ago, she had taken several self-defense classes, but her diminutive size was most definitely a disadvantage in this situation. Still, she prepared herself for a fight, opening her mouth to scream like a banshee at the same time.

Before she could let out a sound, someone else appeared in the alley. Moving with a swiftness that made the bigger man seem to be stuck in slow motion, the newcomer grabbed Jessica's arm and shoved her roughly out of the way, his eyes never leaving the bigger man's face.

"You want a *real* fight?" the man who had followed Jessica into the pharmacy demanded, his entire body braced for battle.

This was the time to get out of here, Jessica decided, climbing to her feet with a wince. She had landed flat on her butt when her rescuer shoved her, and she was a bit sore, but not so badly hurt she couldn't run. Keeping an eye on the two men engaged in a snarling measuring match only a few feet away, she looked frantically around for her big red tote bag. She couldn't leave it behind. It held everything that was of particular importance to her just now.

On her knees, she leaned to look under a Dumpster. Spotting her canvas tote bag beneath the wheels, she dived forward to fish it out, snagging a handle and yanking it toward her. Cursing when the bag caught on something, she used both hands to pull, nearly tumbling over backward when it came loose.

Someone steadied her from behind. Clutching the bag to her chest, she scrambled around and to her feet, not sure whether she was relieved to see the man she had first spotted in the pharmacy. There was no sign now of the big guy who had accosted her. Apparently, he'd had no interest in fighting someone closer to his own size.

Holding both hands up in a gesture meant to reassure her, her rescuer asked, "Are you all right?"

She was already sidling away from him. "I'm fine."

"I'm sorry I made you fall. I didn't mean to push you so hard."

"Just stay away from me."

Though she couldn't see his eyes behind his dark glasses, she had the distinct impression they narrowed in response to her tone. "You're welcome," he muttered.

"I'm supposed to be grateful that you've been following me for weeks?" she snapped, hugging the bag more tightly.

That shut him up—but only for a moment. "I don't know what you're talking about."

"Right." She turned away. "And I suppose you aren't working for my father, either."

He didn't say a word as she walked away. At the end of the alley, she looked over her shoulder to say, "If I see you again, I'll call the police and charge you with stalking me."

She made her escape before he could reply, hoping he would admit defeat now that she had identified him. That was usually the pattern of the men her father hired to keep watch over her. The only reason she hadn't confronted this guy before was because he would only be replaced with someone she might not be able to identify so quickly.

Better the devil she sort of knew...

Sam Fields didn't give up quite so easily. Though it galled him that Jessica had spotted him often enough to know he had been tailing her—how the hell had she done that, anyway?—his irritation simply made him more determined to do a better job in the future.

He was confident that she didn't see him watch her meeting with Derek Ross that afternoon.

As he had predicted, she had rushed back to her place after their confrontation in the alleyway to change out of the clothes she'd soiled in her fall. Parked outside the estate walls where she couldn't see him, he had changed his own appearance while she'd freshened up.

He had ditched the cap and wig to reveal his own shaggy, dark blond hair, swapped his dark sunglasses for glasses with brown plastic rims and thick, clear lenses and shed his flannel shirt to reveal the long-sleeved Cal Tech T-shirt beneath. He replaced his ragged denim jacket with a V-neck sweater, and his dirty boots with a pair of brown loafers. He ran some pomade through his hair, slicking it back and making it look darker than his usual gold. That quickly, he changed from grubby street guy to young businessman on a day off.

When Jessica met Derek Ross at a dimly lit café in downtown San Francisco, Sam was in a nearby booth, his back turned to them. He was able to see them in a wall mirror, but he positioned himself so they couldn't see him in return.

Jessica wasn't making him this time, he promised himself.

He didn't know why he was being so persistent with this case. Yeah, sure, the money was good and his private investigation agency could certainly use the infusion of capital. But damn it, his client was in jail and the woman he was supposed to be watching was…well, Jessica Parks was a kook. Impulsive, unpredictable, temperamental. Always getting into trouble.

One expected artists to be that way, of course—at least from what Sam had observed over the years. But Jessica took eccentricity to new heights, according to her father. She had been getting into scrapes since she was a kid, enough that her family worried about her emotional stability. Apparently, her mother had been the same way, ending up committed to a mental institution for the past twenty-five years.

Maybe Jessica had inherited her mother's emotional problems, but Sam couldn't help wondering if the inclination for shoplifting he had been warned about had been passed down from her father. After all, Walter Parks was facing a preliminary hearing for a variety of charges, including gem smuggling, embezzlement—and murder.

While Parks fiercely maintained his innocence, claiming to have been set up by the enemies he had made during his climb to fortune and power, he insisted that his primary concern in hiring Sam had been Jessica's safety. He worried about his youngest child, with everything so chaotic and unsettled in their family, he had told Sam. Jessica didn't handle change and pressure well. She tended to respond by reverting to behavior that had plagued her in the past—shoplifting, sleepwalking, paranoia, even memory lapses.

Walter also expressed concern that his money made her a target for unscrupulous opportunists—as it had when she had been kidnapped eight years ago and held two weeks until Walter had paid a ransom. The kidnappers had never been captured, and Walter said it had been a miracle that Jessica wasn't harmed. He didn't want to tempt fate again, he insisted.

Walter seemed particularly disturbed by Jessica's recent friendship with Derek Ross, the brother-in-law of an old business partner of Walter's—the partner Walter was now accused of murdering. Walter had confided in Sam that Ross had once had a romantic interest in Jessica's beautiful, but unbalanced, mother. It worried him that Ross seemed to be cultivating an acquaintance with Jessica—what was the lying cheat up to now?

Jessica had long been obsessed with her mother, unable to accept that Anna Parks was too deeply disturbed to live without constant supervision. Of course, it was only natural that with her father ripped from his family and her siblings all very recently married, Jessica would focus on her long-absent mother, Walter had added plaintively.

Sam risked another glance at the mirror. Behind him in the café, Jessica and Ross were deep into a low-voiced conversation, neither touching the rapidly cooling cups of coffee in front of them. Sam would like to know what they were talking about. He didn't trust the way the older guy was looking at Jessica.

Sure, she was hot—as Sam had noticed way too many times, himself—but young enough to be Ross's daughter. Walter said Ross had once had a thing for Jessica's mother, whom Jessica was said to closely resemble. Surely the old guy wasn't turning his romantic attentions to this younger copy of his onetime love?

Repelled by the idea, Sam scowled into his own mug.

It was bad enough that *he* had to fight an unwelcome attraction to Jessica, and he was only twelve years her senior. Ross had to be more than twenty years older. Gross.

Wasn't any of Sam's business, of course—his job for now was simply to keep Jessica safe and out of trouble while her father was away. With his money, influence and crack legal team, Walter was justifiably confident about his chances of beating the twenty-five-year-old charges against him.

Still, Sam wondered whether he should quit. Walk away from the dysfunctional family and their money and let someone else take on their problems. Someone Jessica couldn't spot so easily, he added with a scowl of self-reproach.

Maybe it was time for him to take another assignment. Tailing a cheating spouse, perhaps, or gathering evidence on a sticky-fingered employee. If he was really lucky, he'd get an insurance fraud case or an interesting background check.

Anything had to be better than baby-sitting a beautiful young blonde who kept his head spinning with a combination of exasperation and unwanted attraction.

"I'm glad you could take the time to meet me today," Caroline Harper told Jessica Friday afternoon, the day after Jessica's meeting with Derek Ross. "I really needed this chance to talk."

Her friend's call had come at a very inconvenient time, when Jessica had been immersed in plans for the secret trip she would be taking soon. Since she had just seen Caroline last week for their shopping outing—

after which Jessica had found the bracelet in her pocket—she had been tempted to make an excuse not to meet at this popular coffee shop. But Caroline was pretty much Jessica's only friend, and she had sounded so blue when she'd called that Jessica hadn't been able to refuse.

"You know I'll always make time for you, Caroline. Haven't you done the same for me, too many times to count?"

Without answering, Caroline gazed down at the spoon she was slowly swirling in an oversize cup of hazelnut coffee. There were many times—such as this one—when Jessica found her friend's strikingly attractive face difficult to read.

On the surface, Jessica and Caroline were quite different. Jessica was five foot four on her tallest days, while Caroline was closer to five-ten. Jessica's figure was slight, but curvy; Caroline seemed to be made up of intriguing planes and angles. Both were blond, but while Jessica's shoulder-length hair was naturally silvery, Caroline's stylishly short cut was more golden, and straight out of a bottle.

They were different in other ways, too. Jessica constantly fought nerves and self-doubt; Caroline was the most implacable and confident person Jessica knew—outside the Parks family, anyway. To Jessica, who had been raised in wealth and privilege and knew how little true happiness either provided, money was simply a means to an end. Caroline was admittedly and unrepentantly materialistic.

After finishing the same art school three years earlier, they had gone separate directions careerwise—Jessica into painting and private showings, Caroline into the faster-paced and higher-paid world of advertising. Yet somehow they had remained friends.

It turned out that Caroline's problem on this afternoon was that her mother had been nagging her to fly home to Ohio for Christmas, which Caroline simply didn't want to do. She had just been back in July for her mother's birthday, she complained, and she had planned to ship her Christmas gifts next week, almost six weeks before the holiday so that they would arrive in plenty of time.

Family problems. Now there was something Jessica understood all too well. "You are her only daughter, after all."

Caroline groaned. "And she never lets me forget it. The only reason she wants me there is to parade me around in front of her friends. She's decided it will make her look bad to her acquaintances if I don't make the effort to come home for the holidays. She's whining and carrying on about her poor health—which is a crock—and her breaking heart—an even bigger crock—and telling me how unnatural and ungrateful I am. You know how it is when a mother gets into wounded-martyr mode."

Jessica's hands tightened a bit convulsively around her own coffee mug. "No, actually. I don't."

Caroline bit her lip. After a moment, she murmured, "Sorry. I wasn't thinking."

Jessica shrugged to indicate she wasn't letting the gaffe bother her. Caroline knew, of course, that Jessica's mother was institutionalized. But not even Caroline knew about Jessica's plan to bring her mother home.

Which only proved that Jessica could lie without flinching to anyone, even her best friend, when she felt it was necessary. When it came to her impending plans, she trusted no one—with the possible exception of Derek Ross.

Caroline sighed. "I'm sorry. I've been rattling on, and I know you've got a lot on your mind. So much has happened in your family. We should talk about how you're doing."

Jessica was very fond of Caroline, who could always be counted on for dry humor, witty observations and total acceptance of Jessica's personality quirks. Caroline was not, however, one who enjoyed deep, emotional discussions or introspective psychological dissections. So, Caroline's occasional questions about the latest soap-operatic developments in Jessica's family were probably prompted more by idle curiosity than genuine empathy.

Jessica could understand that. She was fully aware that her family had kept the tabloid gossips practically salivating during the past year. "I'm fine."

Caroline looked vaguely dissatisfied with the noncommittal response. "Come on, Jess, it helps to talk, sometimes—how do you really feel about what's happening?"

Jessica's mouth twisted. "Depends on what you're referring to. My father being in jail, charged with embezzlement and the murder of his onetime business partner? Or my oldest brother, Cade, a formerly conservative widower and single father, recently eloping with the daughter of the man my father is accused of murdering? Or maybe you're alluding to my only sister, Emily, marrying a European ruler and moving to his country to bear his child and to live as royalty."

Caroline shook her head. "Any of those things are enough to upset you."

But Jessica wasn't finished. "Don't forget that terrible time a few months ago when we thought my brother Rowan had died in a motorcycle accident, only to find out that he was living on a cattle ranch in Texas. Now *he's* gotten married to the mother of an adorable baby boy, leaving me the only single sibling—the one everyone thinks is emotionally unbalanced, by the way.

"And I haven't even mentioned my twenty-four-year-old half brothers, Tyler and Conrad Carlton, who just appeared out of the blue and announced that they were conceived during an affair my father had with the wife of the same man he is now accused of murdering. So they're Cade's half brothers and his wife's half brothers, which is really just too bizarre, when you think about it. I can't imagine why I would walk around these days feeling as if my head is going to spin right off my shoulders, can you?"

Caroline winced. "When you put it that way, my family annoyances don't seem half as bad. Yours sound like a daytime soap opera."

Jessica sighed gustily and shook her head. "Sorry. I didn't mean to unload on you. It's just that everything is so crazy right now."

"I understand. And it's enough to put anyone on edge. Maybe you should just hole up and rest awhile. You could paint, read, watch your favorite DVDs—at least until your father's out of jail."

Jessica had no intention of telling her friend that she planned to make good use of the time her father was away by slipping off, herself. But she couldn't resist commenting, "You make it sound as if there's no question that my father *will* be out of jail."

Caroline lifted one narrow, arched eyebrow. "Really, Jess, as often as you've complained about your father being controlling, distant and critical, you've never implied he could be capable of murder. Maybe he wouldn't be above a little creative accounting or a few shady business practices, but murder?"

Jessica would have given anything to look her friend in the eye and state with absolute confidence that she did not believe Walter Parks was capable of such a deed. But the truth was, she *couldn't* say that. Not after talking to Derek Ross. And not knowing what Walter had done to her mother.

"Jessica?" Caroline looked startled by her continued silence. "You don't think—"

"I don't know what I think," Jessica said wearily. "I told you, I'm too confused to think. For now, I'm just going to trust the courts to sort everything out and find the truth."

"He really does worry about you. As much as you complain about his overprotectiveness, it shows he cares. That's more than my long-absent father ever did for me."

Caroline didn't know, of course, exactly how closely guarded and totally controlled Jessica had been, and this wasn't the time to get into it. But Jessica increasingly doubted that love had anything to do with Walter's actions.

After a moment, Caroline sighed lightly and reached for her purse. "I've got to run. My calendar's full for the rest of the afternoon. Thanks for meeting me. I needed the break."

Jessica forced a smile and accompanied her friend to the cash register. A display of pretty, whimsical refrigerator magnets caught her attention, and she studied them while Caroline paid. Caroline had insisted on treating. And then Caroline turned to give her a quick hug and an air kiss aimed at her cheek. "See you later, kid. Don't do anything crazy, okay? Everything will work out."

Jessica was left to wonder what Caroline had meant by that "don't do anything crazy" crack. Maybe she was a little sensitive about such things, but the remark seemed particularly grating considering her mother's predicament.

Still replaying the conversation with Caroline, she stepped absently onto the sidewalk. Caroline was already gone, having headed in the opposite direction.

"'Don't do anything crazy,'" she muttered, tucking her ever-present tote bag beneath her arm and stepping onto the crosswalk. "I wonder how she would classify flying off to Switzerland to break my mother out of a mental institution. I wonder if she would consider that cr—"

A sudden squeal of brakes—much too close for comfort—drowned out her grumbling. Before Jessica even had a chance to look around, something hit her hard from behind and sent her flying.

Chapter Two

She landed hard on her hands and knees. Jolting pain shot up both her arms and her legs, and her palms felt as though they had just been shredded.

The smell of warm, oily asphalt assaulted her nostrils, making her grimace as she imagined what that fall had done to her good tan slacks. It was a frivolous thought, of course, considering that she had apparently come very close to being hit by a car, but she latched on to the mundane concern for her clothes—all in all, much better than remembering the shrill squeal of brakes and the sick certainty that she was about to be run down in the street.

Voices were raised around her, and a car door slammed as someone shouted, "Dude, she walked right out in front of me! I never even saw her."

Someone gripped her shoulders. "Are you okay?"

Shaking her head slightly as if to clear her addled thoughts, she looked up—straight into a pair of bright green eyes she knew much too well. "Damn it."

It was that guy again—the one who had been following her. The one who had rescued her from a menacing hulk in an alleyway—after putting her into the situation in the first place, she reminded herself defensively.

"Are you all right?"

She remembered his voice, too. For someone so irritating to have such a deliciously deep, rumbly voice was just entirely unfair. "I'm fine," she said curtly. "Now get away from me."

His eyes narrowed, but before he could snap back at her a young man with greasy hair and an unfortunate complexion stepped into her view. "You walked right in front of me, yo," he accused her. "I almost hit you. You know what that would have done to my insurance rates?"

The man who had knocked her out of the path of the car turned his irritation toward the young driver. "Do you know what it would have done to *her?*" he demanded. "You were driving too fast and you weren't paying attention. You could have killed her."

"Hey, it ain't my fault that she's too dumb to read the Don't Walk signs."

The man started to rise, but Jessica placed a hand on his arm. "It was *my* fault," she said loudly and clearly. "I was distracted and I made a stupid mistake. I'm so sorry I frightened you," she told the driver—who couldn't have been more than nineteen.

He started to retort, but then he seemed to pause and study her face for the first time. A flush began somewhere in the vicinity of his prominent Adam's apple and traveled up to his shaggy brown bangs. "Well—that's okay. I guess I'm glad you weren't hurt."

"Thank you." Ignoring her seemingly habitual rescuer, she held out a hand to the young man. She wasn't above using the fragile blue-eyed blonde bit when it was to her benefit—a trick she'd been told she'd inherited from her mother. "Would you mind?"

Blushing even more brightly, the teen helped her awkwardly to her feet. "Is there anything I can do for you?" he offered. "Can I give you a lift, maybe?"

"No, thank you." She gave him a warm smile that had his Adam's apple doing an Irish jig in his throat. "It's very kind of you to offer, but I'll be fine. We'd better move along now, we seem to be causing a scene. Goodbye."

He moved somewhat reluctantly to the ancient sedan he'd pulled haphazardly to the curb after the near collision. Jessica tucked her tote bag beneath her arm and limped to the other sidewalk, relieved that the gawking bystanders moved on when they decided that there would be no further entertainment from her.

It annoyed her greatly that Green Eyes stayed close to her side as she walked away. "You landed pretty hard," he said, an unnecessary reminder since her knees throbbed with every step. "Maybe you should let someone check you out?"

"I believe I've been checked out quite enough for one day, thank you." She was aware that it was a lame response, but it was the best she could come up with at the moment.

"You're limping."

"I'll get over it. Please go away."

"Look, I'm just trying to make sure you're okay. It isn't as if I expect undying gratitude or anything—even though I did push you out of the path of a car—but the least you could do is be civil."

"Civil?" She whirled then to glare at him. "I'm sorry, did I miss an etiquette lesson along the way? Something about being 'civil' to stalkers?"

His cheeks darkened, but unlike the teenager's, this flush was due more to anger than embarrassment. Jade flames snapped in his eyes when he spoke. "I am not a stalker."

"I know exactly what you are," she answered him evenly, holding his gaze and hoping she gave him no sign that she was just a teensy bit intimidated by the way his handsome face hardened when he was mad. Made him look sort of dangerous—a word she hadn't applied to him before. "When you report this incident to my father—as I'm sure you will—tell him that I would rather be hit by a bus than to see your face again. Have I made myself clear?"

"Very." He pushed the single word out from between clenched teeth. And then he turned without another word and disappeared into the crowd—which was quite a trick, considering that there weren't that many people around at the moment.

Because rudeness didn't come naturally to her, Jessica was feeling rather guilty about the things she had said to the green-eyed man by the time she returned to the solitude of her own home. As had become her habit, she didn't even glance at the opulent stucco mansion she drove past on the way to her guest cottage in back.

She had been under some pressure from her siblings to move into the main house now that her father was in jail, but she much preferred her cozy cottage to the fifteen-room showplace in which she had been raised. She didn't want to have to deal with the minimal staff still residing in the mansion, preferring the privacy of her own rooms. Nor did she trust anyone on that staff—with the exception of housekeeper Brenda Wheeler, who was currently away on leave—not to report her every movement to her father.

As far as Jessica was concerned, her father had simply traded the high walls and massive iron gates of his estate for a less luxurious prison.

Once inside her cottage, she headed straight for a hot bath to soak away the aching reminders of her close encounter with the pavement, berating herself all the way for not handling the entire situation a bit differently.

"I should have pretended not to recognize him," she said aloud, stripping off her green cardigan. "Or maybe I should have been icily polite, thanking him for coming to my rescue yet again—the condescending-royalty-to-lowly-peasant routine. Made a comment about my father getting his money's worth from this minion—and maybe I should have offered him a nice tip for his trouble. That would have gotten his goat, without making me sound quite so—"

Her voice faded into shocked silence when her sweater fell to the bathroom floor and a whimsical refrigerator magnet rolled out of the big patch pocket on the left side.

Shaped like a colorful clown, the magnet seemed to laugh mockingly up at her as she stared down in disbelief. She specifically remembered studying that very magnet at the cash register earlier. She'd thought the twelve-dollar price tag was a bit steep for such a paltry trinket, but she hadn't particularly wanted it, anyway. She would have sworn she had put it back on the display rack, not in her pocket. She absolutely didn't remember stashing it there—

But then she had walked into the path of an oncoming car without noticing that, either, she reminded herself in despair.

She wrapped her arms tightly around her middle. Maybe she really was going crazy. Everyone kept telling her she was just like her mother—and everyone said her mother was unstable. Jessica had been trying to prove "everyone" wrong, based on a few letters from her mother that had seemed so sensible and sane—but maybe she had allowed herself to be misled by her lifelong longing for the mother she'd never had the chance to know.

Maybe Anna Parks really was crazy—and maybe she had passed that trait to her youngest daughter.

Dashing a scraped hand across her damp eyes, Jessica lifted her chin, sniffed defiantly and promised herself that very soon, she would have the answer to at least one of her questions. When she looked directly into her mother's eyes, she would know the truth.

"So she would rather be hit by a bus than to see my face again." Sam Fields glared at Jessica's cottage from his parking space in a nearby wooded area. The woods partially concealed the groundskeepers' gate at the back of the mansion, a gate which was kept locked, but to which Sam had been given access by the estate's owner.

The spot where he had been instructed to park was where the groundskeeper kept his truck when he was working on the meticulously landscaped property. There had been little grounds maintenance during the past month since Walter's arrest, leaving Sam free to make use of the space, which turned out to be a convenient position for spying on the cottage. Because that phrase bothered him, he mentally corrected it—it was a convenient position for keeping guard over the cottage, he thought, somewhat more satisfied with the way that sounded.

Though he was too far away to see into her windows, he knew Jessica was still there—her car hadn't moved since she had returned from the luncheon that had almost ended in tragedy more than two hours earlier.

He had made sure she'd gotten home safely, and he had been watching her place ever since, though for what purpose he couldn't quite say. She was certainly safe enough here on the Parks estate, with its walls and gates and vigilant staff—who had, very likely, been instructed to ignore him if they saw him. He had better things to do than to baby-sit an eccentric young woman whose father—his employer—could very well be a murderer, for all Sam knew.

He was beginning to suspect why Walter Parks had felt his youngest child needed a baby-sitter—face it, the woman was an accident waiting to happen—but damned if Sam intended to keep rescuing her from one misadventure after another while Walter awaited his trial.

He really should quit. Walk away, refund a part of the retainer he'd already spent, forget all about Walter Parks and his kooky daughter. Problem was, he wasn't sure it was going to be all that easy to accomplish the latter.

What was it about Jessica Parks that was keeping him on this case? It couldn't be just her beauty. As a divorce-burned, fiercely confirmed bachelor, he knew better than to let himself be captured by a pretty face, at least for more than a brief fling.

Had to be that annoyingly soft heart of his, the one he had spent years trying to harden. He had always been a sucker for a lost or wounded stray, and something about Jessica definitely brought those images to mind. There was something in her eyes…something in the depth of emotion he saw in her paintings…something that made him wonder if he was losing his grip on reality, too, damn it.

Her father was in jail, facing a lifetime sentence. Her siblings all seemed to be too busy with their own hectic affairs to make much time for the little sister who had always been regarded as a bit of a problem in the family. Perhaps they all thought she was safe enough in her cottage on the Parks estate—maybe they even thought she was content there. He knew better, on both counts.

Walter hadn't expressed undue concern about any of his other offspring, but they seemed to be doing fine on their own, as far as Sam could determine. The only other daughter, Emily, had recently married European royalty, so her welfare was certainly guaranteed. Emily's twin brother, Cade, was overwhelmed with responsibilities since Walter's arrest—in addition to raising his five-year-old daughter, and his recent marriage to the daughter of Walter's late ex-partner. The younger brother, the one just ahead of Jessica in birth order, was also a newlywed who had shown little connection to his family, on the whole.

Two other brothers had recently surfaced, twin boys born out of an affair between Walter Parks and his late partner's wife almost twenty-five years ago. Their mother had died recently, and they seemed determined to make Walter Parks pay for the shabby way he had treated her in the past. They, of course, barely knew Jessica and certainly had no emotional ties to her.

He didn't doubt that Jessica felt lonely and isolated now—which Walter had cited as the reason for her renewed obsession with her crazy mother. An obsession that was apparently leading her into an odd alliance with her mother's ex-lover, a man Walter had described as "dangerously unpredictable."

Between that development and her propensity for walking into secluded alleys and oncoming traffic, it certainly seemed as though Jessica needed a bodyguard. Walter said he had tried on numerous occasions to obtain one for her, but she had refused, making him feel it necessary to hire someone to watch out for her on the sly. At least until he was released from jail to take the job back, himself.

"I've been a lousy father, Fields," he had admitted with a candor some might have found disarming. "I didn't pay nearly enough attention to my children when they were growing up, leaving them to be raised by a housekeeper while I devoted all my time to my business.

And now the repercussions of my success have brought this shame to the family. I'm trying to do all I can to make it up to them, in the best way I know how. In Jessica's case, that means keeping her safe and protected from her own fragile nature until I'm in a position to get the best help for her."

Since Parks had made a big deal of being a model prisoner, casting himself in the role of long-suffering martyr whose only purpose was to accomplish as much good as possible while waiting for the justice system to discover his innocence, Sam had reserved judgment about the old reprobate's sincerity. Apparently the D.A. had some strongly incriminating evidence that would be brought out in the preliminary hearing later this month—not to mention a couple of rumored surprise witnesses.

But as far as Jessica needing to be looked after—well, that seemed to be something no one could accuse Parks of exaggerating by much.

Still, none of this was Sam's problem. After all, Jessica recognized him now, which made his job even more difficult, if not impossible. She had said herself that she would rather be mowed down by a bus than see him again.

Some guys might have considered that a pretty strong hint.

Yet every time he thought about quitting, he found himself remembering the moment he had watched Jessica step off a sidewalk and into mortal danger. His heart had leaped into his throat as he had thrown himself at her, not at all sure he would be able to reach her in time, or to keep himself from being flattened with her.

If he had quit last week, as he had been so strongly tempted to do, would she even now be lying in the city morgue?

The image that question brought to his mind almost made him shudder.

"What's this I hear about you refusing to spend Thanksgiving with any of your siblings?" Walter Parks demanded Saturday morning, the day after Jessica's near accident. He made no attempt to mask his annoyance or his disapproval with her holiday plans—or lack thereof.

Jessica sighed heavily into the telephone handset. "Even from jail you're trying to run my life?"

"Don't expect me to be here much longer," he snapped. "My lawyers will have me out of here by the end of the month—and then you and I are going to sit down and talk."

"You sound awfully confident for a man facing as many charges as you are."

He harrumphed, dismissing those charges just as easily as he had always dismissed anything that inconvenienced him—including his children, Jessica thought bitterly. Especially his youngest daughter, the one who had always openly challenged him the most. The one who looked and acted so much like the problematic wife he had banished from his life twenty-five years ago.

"Maybe I'll pay a steep fine, but they aren't going to put me away for making a little extra profit here and there. Everyone knows how the world of cutthroat business operates."

"And the…other charges?" She couldn't seem to make herself say the word *murder*.

"They have nothing," Walter said flatly. "Their so-called witness will be exposed for the lying weasel he is. As I said, I'll be out by the end of the month. In the meantime, I'm doing the best I can to take care of my affairs—and my family—from this cell."

"I assume by taking care of family, you're referring to having me followed everywhere I go?"

"If I *were*," he replied cagily, "it would be for your own good. With me here and you living there on the estate by yourself, you're much too easy a target. You think no one would consider taking advantage of our situation to snatch my youngest child for ransom? Again?" he added, heavily stressing the word.

She was instantly transported eight years back in time, to the two nightmarish weeks she had spent locked in a tiny room while her kidnappers negotiated a ransom with her father. Miraculously, she had been released unharmed, but it had been a long time before she had recovered from the ordeal—not that she had ever fully recuperated.

For more than a year afterward she had been subdued and withdrawn, abandoning the secret plans she had been so close to completing, willing to let her father take charge "for her own sake." A week after her return, Walter had confronted her with a letter from her mother that he had found hidden among her possessions, and he demanded to know how long she had been in contact with Anna. When she sullenly admitted that she had located and contacted her mother a year earlier, he had gone off on a tirade about how unstable and unreliable Anna was, and how Jessica was just like her.

Acting foolishly had almost gotten her killed, he reminded her—which she most certainly would have been if he hadn't sacrificed and paid the exorbitant ransom for her.

After that he had placed even tighter controls on her, restricting her money to absolute necessities, having her watched almost constantly, forbidding her to have any further contact with the mother who was such a horrible influence over her even from so far away. For just over a year, she had gone along, drifting aimlessly until she had impulsively entered art school.

Her obsession with the past and her concerns about her own problems had interfered with her studies, and she hadn't really concentrated on her art. Her teachers had insisted that she had more talent than she allowed them to see, but her heart wasn't really in the process then. Her work had been competent, but not inspired, just enough for her to get by in her classes.

It was her budding friendship with classmate Caroline Harper that had helped her restore some of her faith in herself. After graduation, she had even defied her father to move out of the estate and into a trendy loft apartment, making her living as a displays designer for a high-end department store.

She had enjoyed that brief period of freedom—until the mugging that had dealt her a sharp setback, reminding her too vividly of her kidnapping ordeal. She had allowed Walter to talk her into moving back to the estate, but into the guest cottage this time. Only then had she really begun to concentrate on her art, finding in it an outlet for all of her pent-up emotions.

Eventually, she'd found the courage to contact her mother in secret again, and in time she began to rebuild her precarious faith in Anna, even as her trust in her father started eroding once more. She had even reached a point where she had wondered if he had been behind that traumatizing kidnapping, and maybe even the purse-snatching incident three years later—just to keep her under his control.

For nearly five years she had wondered if he would really go that far, or if she was simply allowing paranoia to get the best of her. She still hadn't convinced herself he wouldn't resort to any coldhearted measure if he felt it necessary. Walter had always taken great pride in his willingness to do whatever it took to serve his own best interests—and those of his children, he had always added belatedly.

Pushing the old fears and self-doubts out of her mind, Jessica lifted her chin and spoke fiercely. "I can take care of myself."

"Not from what I've been hearing," her father answered, his tone familiarly cutting.

She cringed. Heaven only knew what Walter had been told by the green-eyed shadow he refused to acknowledge hiring. Did he know she had walked in front of a car? Her knees still throbbed from their hard contact with the pavement, as did her scabbed palms.

And then her breath caught as something even more unnerving occurred to her. Could Walter possibly know about the shoplifted items that kept showing up in her possession?

She was stressed, she assured herself. Not unstable. Lots of people became distracted under extreme stress, and she was definitely dealing with that condition. She would not let her father shake her self-confidence—or her resolve—again. After all, what could he possibly do to her now?

Before she could try to defend herself, he changed the subject. "Why won't you join your brothers or sister for Thanksgiving?"

"I'm not in a particularly festive or thankful mood this year. Besides, they're all busy with their new lives. I'll be fine by myself."

"I should have refused to give Brenda this time off. At least you'd have her to keep you company."

"Absolutely not. Brenda deserved a long holiday. I hope she has a wonderful time on her European cruise. It was my idea, after all."

"So I assumed," he grumbled.

She didn't tell him, of course, that she had wanted his longtime housekeeper, and the woman who had served as her surrogate mother, out of the way for the next few weeks. As much as she loved Brenda Wheeler, Jessica didn't want to risk any interference with her perilous plans, even from someone who truly did have only her best interests at heart.

"So maybe you'll come see me on Thanksgiving—since you don't have any other obligations."

"Come see you? In prison?" She was startled that he had even suggested it.

"We're allowed visitors, you know." He sounded peevish now. "Not that you've ever taken advantage of it. I'd like to see you, Jessie. I miss my family."

"I, um, really don't want to see you there," she said awkwardly. "It's too…painful for me."

Which was only partly true. She didn't want to see him at all for the time being—not until after she had accomplished her mission.

He wasn't satisfied by her lame response, but she gave him little chance to argue. Muttering a barely coherent excuse, she hastily disconnected the call.

Chapter Three

"Monica, this is fantastic. I can't believe how much you've developed your talent in such a short time."

Jessica gazed in satisfaction at the oil painting propped on an easel in front of her, her hands on her hips as she studied the bold, cleverly layered colors. "The power of this painting is almost palpable. It's as though I can almost feel waves of energy radiating from it."

The spiky-haired, multipierced Monica rolled her black-lined brown eyes. "You do get kinda carried away sometimes."

Jessica chuckled. "Art is supposed to carry you away. Good art, anyway. And yours is better than merely good."

Though she shrugged and muttered gruffly, the teenager couldn't entirely hide her pleasure with the compliments. Jessica doubted that Monica had heard many

compliments during her short life. Because Jessica
could identify with that, and with Monica's need to seek
attention in ways that were sometimes self-destructive,
she wanted very badly to be a positive influence in the
girl's life.

Jessica had been lucky enough to have Brenda Wheeler,
a loving and vigilant housekeeper, on her side. Monica had
no one except the overworked staff and volunteers at this
facility for troubled teenagers. Which was why Jessica was
hesitant to tell her she was going out of town. "I'd like you
to keep working on your paintings for the next few weeks.
I won't be here for the next couple of Wednesdays, but I'll
get back as quickly as I can to see what you've done and
teach you some new techniques, okay?"

The girl's square, acne-spotted face hardened.
"You're quitting?"

"I'm not quitting my volunteer work here," Jessica
replied firmly. "I simply have to take a couple of weeks
off for family business."

"Holiday stuff, I bet," a painfully thin boy said from
nearby, where he was working on a clay sculpture that
Jessica privately thought more closely resembled an
aardvark than the Corvette he had proclaimed it to be.
"Next week's Thanksgiving. Folks with normal families
get real busy between Thanksgiving and Christmas. Unlike us defectives," he added with a wry look at Monica, "who'd rather spend the holidays in a smelly alley
than with the weirdos we got for relatives."

He had no idea, of course, how painful his words
were to Jessica. Her relatives weren't exactly weirdos—
at least, her siblings were all sane enough—but she

could hardly call hers a "normal" family. Not considering where her parents were at the moment, one in jail, the other in a mental institution.

"I'll be back," she assured them and the other four scruffy teenagers working with various degrees of enthusiasm on projects in the classroom-turned-studio. "I promise."

She hoped that by the next time she saw them, there would be some major changes in her own life. Maybe then she could concentrate more fully on helping them make much-needed changes in their own.

Monica was clearly not happy about Jessica's plans to miss a couple of Wednesdays, but she would not openly admit that she had come to depend upon and enjoy these informal art classes. Jessica hoped her plans didn't interfere with the girl's therapy, which was progressing very slowly, but she couldn't let herself be distracted even by that important consideration.

She had come too far with her plans to take any chance of being thwarted again, for any reason.

"Yo, Fields. Where the hell you been for the past month?"

Sam turned slightly on his bar stool to acknowledge the stocky, bristle-haired, recently retired cop who slid onto the next stool. It was Wednesday evening, and Sam had left Jessica safely tucked into her bungalow, where he had seen the studio lights burning ever since she had returned from her volunteer gig. It felt good to have a free evening without having to worry about Miss Walking Disaster.

"Hey, Ed. What's going on?"

"I asked first. Where you been?" As he spoke, Ed motioned to the bartender and pointed to Sam's beer to indicate he would have the same.

"Busy."

"Work busy or play busy?"

Sam chuckled wryly. "Definitely work."

"Too bad. I thought maybe you'd gotten involved with a rich, gorgeous blonde and left all this behind."

Sam's eyebrows shot up. "What have you heard?"

Lifting his foaming mug to his lips, Ed paused. "I was just joking. Why? *Is* there a rich, gorgeous blonde?"

Shaking his head impatiently at his own uncharacteristic quickness to jump to conclusions, Sam replied, "Many of them. I just haven't found one willing to put up with me yet. In fact," he added with a slight smile, "the last one I talked to informed me she would rather walk in front of a bus than to see my face again."

That made his old friend laugh. "Ain't no surprise there. You do have a face that would scare a hungry grizzly back into his cave."

Automatically, Sam glanced at the mirror behind the bar. His own familiar face gazed back at him, a bit grimmer than usual, but still ordinary enough, in his opinion. His ex-wife had called him "good-looking—in an average Joe sort of way." He had never figured out if it was a compliment, but not being the vain type, he hadn't wasted much time worrying about it.

"So what are you working on now? Or can you tell me?"

Ed had always been curious about the small-time private investigation business Sam had started a couple of years ago after leaving the San Francisco police department. Still smarting from his ugly divorce—and still humiliated at having learned afterward that his cop-groupie ex-wife had slept with several of his co-workers—Sam had wanted a job that let him be his own boss, set his own hours and interact with other people as little as necessary.

Money hadn't been an issue. Sam's needs had always been simple, and he figured meals into his expenses when he billed the rich clients who appreciated his prudence about their business. The interest from a trust fund left by his maternal grandparents gave him a little cushion, but he would likely never be rich. That wasn't one of his goals.

When clients wanted to look important, they took their security concerns to the high-profile investigation firms. When their concerns were more personal and private, discreet word of mouth led them to Sam. He made it clear from the outset that he didn't break the law—though he'd been known to dip his toes into the shallow waters that marked the line—and he didn't talk, not even to the point of listing previous clients on his professional résumé.

So Ed's asking about his latest case came more from wistfulness than expectation; he knew Sam wouldn't give him any juicy details. "Can't discuss it, except to say that I'm sort of a bodyguard at the moment."

Ed grumbled into his beer. "You can trust me, you know."

"With my life," Sam replied without hesitation. And then added, "But not with the details of my assignments. You know that."

"Yeah, I know," Ed conceded with a slight sigh. "That was one of your problems on the job. You wouldn't even share your files with your fellow officers."

Sam shrugged. "What can I say? I've never been a team player."

"Just like your old man."

Sam winced. He never cared to be compared to his father, a longtime beat cop with a fondness for whiskey and women, and who had died ten years ago when a speeding drunk had mowed him down in front of his favorite bar at midnight. He'd had enough of those comparisons from his embittered mother, who had passed away three years ago still mourning the man she had divorced by law but had never banished completely from her heart.

"You know, this retirement life is pretty damn boring," Ed muttered, staring morosely at his own aging reflection. "When a man's used to having somewhere to go and something to do every day, it ain't easy getting out of bed when there's no reason to do so."

Ed's wife had died last year, and Sam imagined that the older man was at loose ends now that mandatory retirement had taken away the job he'd loved. "You should find something new to occupy your time," he offered awkwardly. "Volunteer work, maybe," he added, remembering Jessica Parks's regular stint at the behavioral facility.

Ed grunted. "Not so easy working for nothing when you're used to drawing a paycheck. Maybe for folks that retire with plenty of money, but a cop's pension doesn't exactly encourage philanthropy. Actually, I was thinking about finding a new job. Maybe some part-time work."

Sam nodded. Ed was only in his midsixties, and in good shape, considering. There was no reason he couldn't find work, assuming a prospective employer would overlook the age thing. "What are you interested in?"

Running a stubby fingertip around the top of his beer mug, Ed cleared his throat. "Thought maybe I could find a small investigation agency that could benefit from the experience of an ex-cop. I'm pretty handy with a computer, you know. Got plenty of experience sitting stakeout."

Oh, hell. Looked as though this friendly exchange had suddenly turned into a job interview. Sam squirmed on his stool, trying to decide what to say. Truth was, there were times he could use some help, as badly as he hated to admit it. And there was no one he trusted more than Ed Armstrong. But he would hate to risk a long-time friendship if a professional collaboration didn't work out.

"Maybe we can talk about it over dinner," he said after a moment. "But you have to remember, I've got a very small operation. There are times when I'm lucky to get paid, much less support anyone else."

"I've got my retirement check to tide me through the lean times. I need the work more than the money. And I've always thought I'd like to try my hand at what you do—me and every other cop on the force," Ed added wryly. "I've had a few friends in the business, and I know it ain't like TV. Mostly routine stuff. But it would be something more productive to do than watch my toe-nails grow. And, damn it, Sam, I need that."

Sam nodded again. It was a plus that Ed wasn't ex-pecting nonstop drama and excitement. There were probably several tasks he could do that would help Sam out immensely. While the thought of being responsible for anyone else weighed heavily on him, he guessed if he had to work with anyone, Ed wouldn't be so bad.

"We'll talk," he promised again, trying to ignore the worry that hiring an employee was the first step toward the life of responsibility and obligation that he had es-caped two years ago.

Satisfied that he had made his case, Ed obligingly changed the subject to the football playoffs while they finished their beers.

Jessica's nerves were stretched almost to the break-ing point during the remainder of that week. She stayed in her cottage much of the time, finalizing her travel plans by computer, trying to burn off energy through her painting.

Her phone rang more often than usual. Caroline called several times, as did Cade and Emily. Perhaps her friend and siblings sensed that Jessica was keeping something from them. Something that made them un-easy—as she so often did. Jessica did her best to con-vince all of them that she was fine, simply busy with several new painting projects for an anticipated show-ing in February.

She hated lying to them, but she didn't trust any of them not to interfere if they found out what she was scheming. Caroline and Emily would be concerned about her, and so would Cade, in his rather bossy and overly responsible manner. She couldn't risk having any of them try to stop her. Or worse, say something to her father.

On the rare occasions when she had to go out, she kept looking warily over her shoulder, trying to spot the man who had been following her. She saw no signs of him, which meant either that he had given up or he had gotten more skilled at hiding from her. She wanted to believe the former, but she had a sinking suspicion that the latter was true. Something in the man's hard jaw and intense green eyes made her doubt that he was the type to give up easily.

That thought led her to an all new attack of anxiety. What if Walter had simply replaced one paid shadow with another one? How did she know there wasn't someone new watching her every move?

Sitting in a coffee shop in the financial district after going by her bank to make a withdrawal—one she hoped her father or brother wouldn't learn about too soon—she eyed the other customers, trying to decide if any of them looked particularly interested in her. Her gaze lingered on the back of a blond man in one corner, but then she relaxed when he turned his head and she saw immediately that it was not the one who had been following her.

Maybe he really had gone away. And maybe her father had decided to forget about having her followed for the time being.

And maybe pigs would fly, she thought with a frown.

"Excuse me, miss?"

Jumping slightly, she turned to look up at the older man standing by the tiny table-for-two where she sat with her latte and newspaper. Ex-military, she would bet, judging from the brush-cut hair and stiff bearing. Older than she would expect for someone hired by her father, but she wasn't ruling him out.

"Yes?" she asked, her tone cool.

"I think you dropped this." He held out a black leather glove. "It was on the floor behind your chair."

Automatically, she checked the pocket of her leather jacket. She dug out a single glove that matched the one he held. "Yes, it is mine," she said, her voice a bit warmer now. "Thank you."

He smiled, then nodded toward the mug in front of her. "Do you mind if I ask what you're having? That looks pretty good on a damp, cool afternoon like this."

"It's a mocha latte. And it is good."

"Maybe I'll try one, then. Have a nice day."

Automatically murmuring a response to the clichéd phrase, Jessica watched him walk away. He never glanced at her again as she finished her latte then gathered her things to leave, making sure she had both gloves this time. Apparently she had let her paranoia run away with her again. This was what her father always did to her, making her constantly question herself and everyone around her.

She hoped before long she would finally have some answers to those lifelong doubts.

She almost got away from him.

Sam didn't know what made him assign Ed to watch Jessica overnight Wednesday, since she rarely left her cottage after 10:00 p.m. or before 8:00 a.m. Something about the increasing secretiveness of her actions—and something about the furtive bank visit Ed had witnessed while tailing her—nagged at him.

Even as he asked Ed to keep an eye on her place from midnight to 7:00 a.m. while Sam got some rest, he wondered just how long he intended to keep this up.

Walter's hearing was scheduled to begin a week from next Monday—the last week in November. Sam's assignment had been to keep an eye on Jessica until then, after which Walter seemed confident he would be free to watch her himself. Even had Sam been more convinced of Walter's chances of walking away from that trial a free man, he wasn't sure he wanted to spend the next two weeks shadowing Jessica, especially this twenty-four hour surveillance he had initiated.

Damn, but he wished it was his commitment to his job—even eagerness for a paycheck—that had him watching out for her, and not an itchy feeling combined with an ever-present awareness of the vulnerability hidden beneath the bravado she had shown to him.

His cell phone rang just as he poured his first cup of coffee Thursday morning. He had already showered and dressed, and thought he had time for breakfast and the newspaper before relieving Ed on Jessica-watch. He'd been wrong.

"She's on the move," Ed reported. "I assume you want me to follow her?"

Startled, Sam looked at his watch. Not even 6:00 a.m. yet. "Where's she headed?"

"Not sure yet. Her car just pulled out of the driveway."

"Stay close enough not to lose her, but far enough back to keep her from spotting you. Remember, she isn't easy to fool."

He was already on the run to his own car, a bad feeling gripping him.

Jessica's heart was pounding so hard she could feel it banging against the wall of her chest. After all the years, all the careful planning, all the lies and anxiety, she was finally going through with the plan she had been making for so very long.

The last time she'd tried this, she had ended up locked in a room that was little more than a closet, certain she was going to die. Eight years later, the trauma of that ordeal still held her in its grasp, but she refused to give in to the fear. She wasn't eighteen and naive anymore, she reminded herself. This time she would be on her guard.

She took a winding route to the Oakland airport—just in case. There wasn't a lot of traffic, though the morning commute had begun. She'd left earlier than necessary to catch her flight, but she wanted to arrive in plenty of time. She'd been too anxious to wait any longer, anyway. She kept looking nervously up at the rearview mirror, but no vehicle in particular caught her attention.

She could have departed from the San Francisco airport, but she didn't want anyone finding her tracks too quickly. To further conceal her plans, she had carried the tickets and her passport in her tote bag everywhere she had gone lately, along with a few letters from her mother. She hadn't let that bag out of her sight for a moment, nor had she allowed the slightest hint of her intentions to escape her when she had talked to Caroline or her siblings.

She'd had to buy the tickets in her own name, of course, considering the state of airport security, but by the time anyone figured out she was gone, she hoped it would be too late to stop her. She could only hope Green Eyes hadn't been on the job this early.

She was prepared to fight him—or anyone else who tried to get in her way this time.

"Sam—she's headed for the airport."

Using the hands-free function of his cell phone, Sam tightened his grip on his steering wheel as he replied, "I'm almost there, Ed. Don't lose her. I'll get back to you."

Disconnecting that call, he placed another. "Got anything yet?" he asked without bothering to identify himself when a woman's voice answered.

"Jessica Parks is booked on the 11:00 a.m. flight to Chicago," Angie Sawyer replied, her rich voice still morning gravelly. "She should land in Chicago at around three this afternoon, our time."

"Why the hell is she going to Chicago?"

"From Chicago, she's headed for Zurich. From Zurich, she's taking a flight to Geneva. Barring delays, it's a trip of about seventeen hours total—and it's nine hours later in Geneva than it is here. Major jet lag ahead."

"Angie, you are a miracle worker," Sam told his old friend with utter sincerity. "I don't know how you do it."

"Let's just leave it at that, shall we?"

Because he suspected there were things about her methods he would be better off not knowing, he merely said, "I owe you."

"Big-time," she agreed. "Is the sun even up yet?"

"I know how you feel about morning, and I promise I'll make it up to you. Now tell me I've got seats on those flights, and I'll be your slave forever."

"You've got seats—and you don't want to know what they're costing you. Hope you've got your passport."

"Yeah, I've got it," he said in relief after scrambling in the glove compartment while trying to drive one-handed at breakneck speed. It would be another miracle if he made it to the airport in one piece, or without being stopped by a patrol car.

As for the expenses—Walter Parks would be picking those up. At least Sam sincerely hoped the old man would find a way to pay the debts he was racking up from jail.

He had little doubt Parks would order him to stay on Jessica's trail, though he wasn't sure what he was supposed to do once he caught up with her. Would Parks want him serving strictly as her bodyguard, or would he expect Sam to somehow try to interfere with her unexpected actions?

Sam had made some dicey business decisions before, but jumping on a plane to Switzerland on such short notice and without a specific plan in mind probably took the cake. Maybe he was taking his bodyguard responsibilities too far this time. Yet the thought of pretty, accident-prone Jessica Parks heading off to Europe on her own for heaven only knew what purpose made his head hurt. Damn it.

Angie seemed to read his mind—a talent he wouldn't put beyond her, since she was rather spooky in her ability to provide him with whatever information he needed on a moment's notice. "You've made last-minute unscheduled trips before, but this might be a record."

"I think you're right." Fortunately he kept a packed bag in his trunk, in addition to the passport in his glove compartment. In his line of work, it was always good to be prepared.

Chapter Four

Sam connected with his client while he was waiting to board, staying well in the background of milling travelers to keep Jessica from spotting him. It was an indication of Walter's wealth and influence that Sam had no difficulty having him summoned to a telephone; he'd simply said it was a family emergency.

"She's leaving the country," he said with little preamble. "She's booked on a flight to Switzerland."

Walter swore roughly through the phone lines. "Stop her."

"It's too late for that. The plane is already boarding."

"Damn it. Ahh—"

Because that sounded suspiciously like a grunt of pain, Sam frowned. "Parks?"

"I'm all right. Stress like this always gives me heartburn. Get on the plane with her, Fields. I don't care how you manage it. I'll pay your fare."

"Already arranged—but what exactly do you want me to do?"

"Keep her safe. And if there's any way on earth you can stop her from meeting with her mother in Lausanne, do it. I'll try to pull some strings from here, but there's only so much I can do under the present circumstances."

"Just why *are* you so opposed to Jessica meeting with her mother?"

"Haven't you been paying attention, Fields? Anna is dangerously unstable—so sick that she's been committed for most of Jessica's life. And Jessica, I'm sorry to say, is very much like her mother. I'm afraid that Anna and her ex-lover will have too much influence over Jessica, feed her a bunch of wild tales that Jessica might very well believe. That's just the sort of thing that could tip my daughter over the edge herself."

"Insanity is not contagious."

What might have been a growl rumbled in Sam's ear. "But it is hereditary. Why do you think I've watched my daughter so closely? You've said yourself that her behavior is erratic. Not to mention the danger of a wealthy, sheltered young woman traveling such a long way alone. The last time she tried to take off like this, she was kidnapped. It was a miracle she wasn't killed."

Sam had never particularly liked this guy—and he sure wouldn't go as far as to say he trusted him—but securing a high-profile client like Walter Parks had been a real coup for Sam's fledgling investigation business. Parks had directed a couple of other jobs his way, which had helped keep him afloat for the past year. Watching out for his daughter during Walter's incarceration had seemed like a simple enough task for a more-than-satisfactory fee.

The most difficult part of the job at the beginning had been Sam's unwelcome attraction to the young woman he was supposed to be objectively shadowing.

"Look, Fields." Walter sounded suspiciously cagey now. "I still have access to a couple of bank accounts the feds haven't frozen yet. I can have a sizable chunk of money transferred into your name with one phone call. All you have to do is keep Jessica safe. The best way would be to keep her away from her crazy mother. Try to get her safely back home and turn her over to her brothers. I'll make the arrangements for her care after that."

Sam suspected he knew exactly what sort of "care" Walter planned to arrange for his youngest daughter. The same sort of care he'd provided her mother for the past twenty-five years, most likely.

Every instinct he possessed was sounding an alarm as this call progressed. Something was seriously wrong, and he had a gut feeling it all originated with the man at the other end of the phone lines. The man who was about to be tried for several serious crimes—including murder.

"I'll take care of Jessica," he said into the phone. "You transfer the money. I'm going to need it. Last-minute trips to Switzerland are a bit out of my usual budget."

"Done." Walter seemed to have no doubt that the promise of payment had just bought him another unquestioningly loyal lackey. "Now, I have to go. I've got some calls to make. You stick close to my girl, and there will be a nice bonus for you if you get her home before midnight tonight."

Sam disconnected the call feeling as though he needed to go wash his hands. Walter Parks could well be the sort of man who would do anything for money, and maybe he thought Sam would, too. But he was wrong.

Sitting seven rows behind Jessica on the plane, Sam watched the back of her head, confident that she hadn't yet spotted him. It was inevitable that she would eventually, of course, if they were going to be traveling together for the next seventeen-plus hours, but he wanted to put the confrontation off for as long as possible.

There hadn't been time to don a disguise—not that he could have flown in disguise, anyway, in this new era of paranoid airport security. He had to settle for a baseball cap pulled low over his dark gold hair and a pair of tinted glasses with mirrored lenses to conceal his eyes.

Lacking anything better to do, he spent a while wondering what it was about him that she had spotted even in disguise. The way he walked, maybe? Something about the way he carried himself?

He'd have to practice walking and standing differently when he was undercover. He'd always been pretty good at it with everyone else, but Jessica had a particularly sharp eye, apparently.

He noticed that she drew a bit of attention from other men on the flight, men who didn't mind passing the time admiring a pretty young blonde. Most of them had the courtesy to be discreet about it, but there were a couple who ogled her with a boldness that made Sam's fists itch.

It wasn't a territorial thing, he assured himself. He had no intention of following up on his own unwanted attraction to Jessica Parks. But as her bodyguard, it was his responsibility to make sure she didn't have to fend off unwelcome advances during her long trip.

At least, that was what he told himself even as he glared at one particularly aggressive guy—a salesman, Sam would guess—who kept leaning across the aisle to make comments to Jessica. She appeared to be responding politely, but with little encouragement.

Sam could have told her that outright rudeness was the only way to get through to jerks like that, but rudeness didn't seem to be an intrinsic part of her nature. Even though she had tried her best to get rid of Sam with angry, cutting remarks, he remembered with a wry half smile.

The woman in the seat beside him apparently interpreted that smile as a signal that he was in the mood for conversation. She made a comment about the bad weather they were flying into, hoping aloud that it wouldn't interfere with her connecting flight to Boston, where she was going to spend the next week celebrating Thanksgiving with her family. Sam responded congenially, but he made no effort to keep the small talk flowing.

A brunette in her midthirties, she had a pleasant face and a musical voice, pretty dark eyes and a figure that was attractive even with the twenty extra pounds she carried. The kind of woman Sam might have flirted with had his concentration not been so focused on his job.

He hadn't looked for anything more than a pleasant evening with a woman since his divorce. Janice had stung him so badly that he couldn't even imagine putting himself into a situation like that again.

Hell, he hadn't really wanted to get married in the first place, but Janice had convinced him it was a good idea—and at first, everything had been just fine. He'd rather liked coming home to a warm meal and a warmer welcome. She'd been a bit of a fanatic about keeping a clean house.

It was only after he'd come home unexpectedly one afternoon to find her in bed with another cop that Sam had realized she was always prepared for company.

Shaking his head impatiently, he plucked a flight magazine from the back pocket of the seat in front of him and buried his face in it. He didn't really care about the articles, but anything beat sitting there thinking about the humiliating end of his short-lived marriage. He didn't know why he was thinking of that today, anyway.

He had a job to do. And not a clue about how he was supposed to do it.

Jessica had planned for every contingency, or so she had believed. The one thing she hadn't been able to predict was the weather.

She had known when she left Oakland that an early snowstorm was predicted in the Midwest. There had been warnings of delays in air travel, but she had taken a chance and left, anyway, afraid that if she didn't go today, she never would. Maybe she would be on the way to Zurich by the time the storm interfered with flights in and out of O'Hare.

But by the time the plane landed in Chicago, the pilot was already preparing them for the possibility that they probably wouldn't be leaving anytime soon. They had to circle for quite a while, so that it was almost four in the afternoon before they were cleared to land.

They were warned that the airport would soon be closed to both incoming and departing flights. Temperatures were expected to warm by the next morning, but because of the heavy snowfall here and also hitting the East Coast, they could expect delays of up to twenty-four hours, the pilot informed them sympathetically.

Groaning, Jessica thought that she wouldn't have put it past Walter to somehow arrange for this storm. Anything to keep her from finally getting to her mother.

"Bummer, isn't it?" The persistently flirtatious man across the aisle caught her eye with a commiserating grimace. "I don't know about you, but an overnight delay will put a serious crimp in my plans."

"Yes, mine, too." She laced her fingers tightly in her lap, trying to reassure herself that everything would still work out. After all, it would take a while for anyone to notice that she was gone.

She had plugged automatic timers into the lamps and the television in her cottage so that it appeared she was staying at home today. She'd dropped hints to her friends and family that she planned to concentrate on her art for a few days, and might not immediately return phone messages. They knew she sometimes holed up in her studio for days at a time, so that behavior wouldn't seem unusual to them now.

Even if her father's hired snoop was still on the job,

he wouldn't necessarily know she wasn't home, she mused. Green Eyes would very likely spend the entire day watching lights go on and off in her cottage windows, a prospect that she found quite satisfying. By the time anyone realized she wasn't home, and by the time they tracked her movements to the Oakland airport, she hoped to already be in Switzerland, her mission well under way.

"It would be a shame to spend all that time bored and at loose ends in the airport, don't you think?" the pushy wannabe Lothario persisted. "Maybe you and I could find something to do to entertain ourselves until the storm clears, hmm?"

"Fortunately, I brought a couple of good books," Jessica replied. "That's all the entertainment I want."

She deliberately turned her shoulder to him. Some men were incredibly slow to take a hint.

For some reason, she found herself picturing a green-eyed man with tumbled dark gold hair and a lazy smile. Even as she thought again that it was terribly unfair for anyone in league with her father to look that darned good, she was greatly relieved that she wouldn't have to deal with him again for the foreseeable future.

Something told her he wouldn't be nearly as easy to brush off as the man across the aisle from her.

The general pandemonium at O'Hare made it easy for Sam to keep an eye on Jessica without her spotting him. He watched as she joined a crowd of frantic travelers trying to persuade airport officials to let their flights take off despite the dangerous conditions, but she conceded more quickly than most, seeming to accept the inevitable delay with gloomy resignation.

Staying well behind her, he followed her to a bank of windows, where she perched on a vinyl bench and watched the snow fall. She clutched her ever-present red tote bag in her arms, and her face was as clouded as the sky outside.

He couldn't help wondering what she was thinking, and what had brought her to this place in this manner. Why had she felt it necessary to sneak away as she had? Why hadn't she been able to turn to her siblings for advice, if not to her father? Did she really feel so alone?

Damn, but she looked pretty sitting there framed in a frosted window, her fair hair reflecting the bright fluorescent lights above her, her big blue eyes dominating her oval face. Maybe if he were a few years younger, and not working for her father, and hadn't been burned by his faithless ex-wife...

"And maybe if frogs had wings," he muttered in disgust, shaking his head. A couple of elderly women standing near him gave him a wary glance and sidled away, obviously unnerved by his grim expression and the fact that he was talking nonsense to himself.

His attention was drawn quickly back to Jessica, and his frown deepened when he saw the pushy guy from the plane—the one Sam had dubbed "Not So Good Time Charley"—edging closer to Jessica's bench. That guy just didn't know when he was crossing the line, Sam thought irritably. And apparently Jessica wasn't doing a very good job of getting the message to him that she wasn't interested in an airport dalliance to pass the time.

As much as she would resent it, maybe it was time for Sam to interfere.

He relaxed against the wall again when the guy spoke to Jessica and she said something in return that had ol' Charley hurrying away with a scowl that indicated he had been firmly rebuffed. So maybe Jessica was better able to take care of herself than Sam had expected. Anyone who looked like that must have had plenty of unwelcome advances in her time. Apparently she had learned to deal with them harshly enough when necessary.

Relieved that he wouldn't have to reveal himself yet, he went back to watching her.

With each passing moment Jessica spent at the airport, she could almost feel her father closing in on her. Paranoid, of course, with him being in jail in San Francisco, but she had learned from hard experience that Walter had a knack for getting his way, despite the obstacles.

Unlike the hundreds of other stranded travelers, she didn't while away the hours exploring the shops and attractions in the airport. She bought expensive airport food at around 6:00 p.m. because she was hungry, but she ate mechanically, barely tasting the meal. She stayed close to the gate where her plane was to depart, almost afraid that if she moved too far away it would leave without her.

She made no effort to find a hotel room for the night, as so many others had done. Maybe she was being superstitious, but she felt as though staying close was her best bet for getting back on track in her mission.

She claimed a spot on the carpeted floor with her

back against a wall and pulled a paperback suspense novel from her tote bag. She buried her face in the book, hoping the fast-paced story would make the time pass more quickly.

Every so often she felt a funny sensation, as though she were being watched. Each time she glanced up surreptitiously to look around, but she didn't notice anyone in particular.

A few bored men tried to catch her eye, maybe hoping the young blonde would want some company, but she made sure she didn't do anything that could be interpreted as encouragement. Using her book as both a diversion and a shield, she forced herself to be patient, when every muscle in her body twitched with the need to be on her way again.

She was more than a little unnerved when a couple of television crews appeared to do a story about the airport shutdown, but she made sure she didn't get anywhere within range of their cameras. Chances were that no one would recognize her in the background of a weather-related news story, but she took precautions, anyway. She was relieved when the crews left, having nothing new to report except that flights were expected to resume the next morning.

As night fell, weary would-be travelers began to look for places to sleep. Every bench and chair was taken, and people stretched out on the floors, using bags for pillows and coats for blankets. Conversation levels, which had been quite loud earlier, fell to a muted buzz. A few whining children and crying babies could be heard in the background, but Jessica was able to tune them out along with the other noises as she pillowed her head on one arm and lay on her side with her back to the wall.

She was glad now that she had dressed comfortably for the flight in a white-trimmed black hoodie and matching fleece pants with sneakers. The fabric wouldn't wrinkle, and it was a comfortable weight even in the drafty terminal.

She was almost afraid to doze, worried that she might miss an important announcement, but she hadn't slept well last night and her eyelids were growing heavy. Letting herself relax as much as possible under the circumstances, she assured herself that she couldn't possibly sleep through a stampede of travelers anxious to board their flights.

Just as she slipped into a restless sleep, she had that eerie feeling again that she was being watched. It wasn't strong enough to make her open her eyes—and besides, for some reason it didn't unnerve her this time. She felt almost as if someone was watching over her, keeping her safe. Smiling a little at her foolishness, she deliberately allowed her mind to go gray.

She woke with a start, her heart racing as if she had been running. It took her a moment to orient herself, and then she tried to relax. Though she couldn't remember the details of her dream, it had been a bad one.

Her restlessly dozing mind had taken her back to the last time she'd tried to leave the country, and the kidnapping that had followed. It was an old nightmare, and one she made every effort not to remember. At least she hadn't woken up screaming this time, she thought in relief, her cheeks burning in humiliation at the very thought.

"Are you okay? You were whimpering."

The concerned question, asked in a husky male voice, made her swallow a groan. Apparently she hadn't been entirely silent during her dream.

"I'm fine, thank you," she said, turning her head toward the man who had scooted next to her to ask. "It was just a bad—"

Her breath caught in her throat and her heart, which had just slowed to a normal pace, began to hammer against her chest again. She could only hope she was still dreaming, still caught in a nightmare from which she would shortly awaken. She didn't want to believe this man was really here with her in this airport so far from San Francisco. "You—"

"Calm down," he said, reaching out quickly to lay a hand on her shoulder. "You don't want to cause a scene at four in the morning. Security will have us both whisked out of this terminal before you finish the first scream."

There was no mistaking that voice. The same deep, rough-edged voice she'd heard several times back in San Francisco—and damn it, in a couple of unwelcome daydreams. She didn't have to guess at the color of the emerald-green eyes hidden behind a pair of lightly tinted glasses, or of the burnished gold hair partially concealed beneath a baseball cap bearing an Oakland Raiders logo.

It was only his very sobering warning about airport security that kept her from shrieking at him. The one thing she did not want to do was to call attention to herself now.

Pushing herself to a sitting position, she shoved her tumbled hair out of her face and hissed at him, "What are you doing here?"

"That's pretty obvious, isn't it? I followed you. We were on the same plane, actually—seven rows apart."

Chagrined that she hadn't noticed him in all the hours that had passed since she'd left that morning, she clenched her hands into fists in her lap. So much for her smugness at getting away unnoticed. All her careful planning, all her secrecy and caution...

"Please tell me you haven't called my father," she found herself almost begging. "Whatever he's paying you, I'll double it," she added recklessly.

She didn't have the money, of course, but she would get it somehow. Whatever it took. "Please..."

"Jessica, I've already called him."

She groaned and closed her eyes, her shoulders sagging. "When?"

"Just before we took off this morning."

"Why has it taken you this long to say anything?"

"Because all I was instructed to do was to watch you. To keep you safe."

"Safe." She said the word on a toneless laugh. "Right. That's all my father wants. For me to be 'safe.'"

"You think there's something more to it?"

She tilted her chin to glare at him. "Would you believe anything I said?"

He hesitated a moment before answering. "Maybe."

At least he hadn't patronized her with a reassuring lie.

"Never mind," she said gruffly, turning her head again. "You work for my father. He's bought your loyalty."

His fingers tightened just a little on her shoulder. "No one buys me."

Maybe there was just a bit too much emphasis in his words. Protesting too much because he knew she was right?

She tried to shrug off his hand. "What are you going to do now? Are you going to try to take me back to San Francisco? Because I swear I'll fight you even if airport security locks us both up."

His sudden smile in response to her fierce whisper would have made her breath catch—had she been able to breathe since she had looked up and recognized him. "As intriguing as that sounds, I don't want to fight you, Jessica. I think it's time for us to talk."

Clutching her tote bag to her chest like a shield, she eyed him suspiciously. "Is it money you want? Because I need what I have with me now, but I swear I'll get you whatever you want if you'll—"

His smile vanished abruptly as he interrupted her. "Damn it, why do you Parkses think everything comes down to cash? I don't want your money. I want some answers."

"I don't understand. Are you working for my father or aren't you?"

"I am. Or I have been."

She didn't know whether to find any encouragement in those words. Clutching her tote more tightly, she asked, "What do you want from me?"

"I told you. I just want to talk."

Looking around the terminal crowded with bodies, both prone and upright, she asked, "Here?"

He followed her glance, then shrugged. "There's a restaurant on the other side of the terminal. The kitchen's closed, but they're letting people sit at the tables and talk. Let's see if we can find a couple of seats there."

She glanced toward the desk, where a weary-looking airline employee was talking on the phone.

"Don't worry, you won't miss any announcements," he reassured her. "The plane won't be taking off for a few hours yet."

She still didn't quite trust him, but she could see no other choice except to go with him. But if he tried anything...anything at all...she would give him the fight of his life, she vowed.

Chapter Five

They found a small table in a back corner of the airport restaurant. Sam even managed to obtain a couple of canned sodas from a vending machine. He handed one to Jessica as he took his seat across from her, and she opened it with the look of someone who craved caffeine.

It was a bit louder in here, since no one was even pretending to sleep. Everyone looked disheveled, tired and a bit grumpy, but at least no one was paying attention to the somber couple in the back corner.

Reminding himself not to be sucked into Jessica's paranoia, Sam ignored everyone else and focused on her pale—but still stunning—face. "Okay, talk."

She lifted one delicately arched eyebrow. "About…?"

"About where you're going. Why you felt the need

to sneak out of your house before dawn. Why your father is so determined to keep you from going."

What might have been bitterness darkened her blue eyes. "Haven't you heard? My father feels the need to protect me from myself. I'm crazy."

Annoyed for some reason, he snapped, "Don't give me that. No one has ever accused you of being crazy."

"Unstable, then. Emotionally fragile."

He couldn't argue with either of those assessments, since that was exactly the way her father had described her. Whether Sam believed it…well, that remained to be seen, and had everything to do with why he had finally decided to approach her after she'd awakened from her bad dream.

"Is that the way you see yourself?" he asked, instead.

She glared at him. "Of course not—even though my father has tried hard enough to convince me otherwise."

"And why would he do that?"

"Isn't it obvious? My father thrives on complete and total control. He wasn't always able to control my other siblings, so he made sure to keep his thumb on me."

"Why you, in particular?"

She ran a fingertip around the top of her soda can, avoiding his eyes as she answered. "I once heard my father tell someone that every time he looks at me he sees my mother looking back at him. It wasn't a compliment."

"Isn't it natural that he would worry about you?" Sam suggested tentatively. "After all, you are his youngest child—and your mother does have problems, apparently…"

Her eyes lifted to his, and the expression in them made his words fade to silence.

"Are you close to your parents, Mr.—I'm sorry, you have me at a disadvantage."

"Sam Fields."

She nodded. She didn't bother to lie that it was nice to meet him, he thought ruefully.

"Are you close to your parents?" she repeated.

"My parents are both dead. But no, we weren't a particularly close family. They divorced when I was just a kid. My father spent the rest of his life pretending his family didn't exist most of the time, and my mother spent the rest of hers trying to keep me from turning into him—with little success, according to her."

That caught her off guard. She studied his face for a long moment before saying, "So you know what it's like to be negatively compared to a parent. It hurts, doesn't it?"

"Yeah," he said, rather surprised at his own candor. "It hurts."

"When you were little—before your parents' marriage fell apart—did they ever tell you they loved you?"

It was hard to remember that far back, partially because he had spent so many years trying not to do so. "Yeah, I guess," he said, wondering how she had managed to turn the conversation to his childhood. "But—"

"My father never said those words to me," Jessica said flatly. "Not once. I don't know if he ever said them to my brothers or sister, but I doubt it. The only person who ever said she loved me was our housekeeper, Brenda Wheeler."

He squirmed in his seat with typically masculine discomfort at the nature of this conversation. "I'm sorry," he said, feeling incredibly awkward. "But—"

"I used to fantasize about my mother," she went on

as if she hadn't heard him. "I told myself she would come back someday and she would be the perfect mother. She would tell me she loved me and she was proud of me and that I was everything she had ever wanted in a daughter. And there would be laughter in our household, and warmth. And maybe she would even make my father happy again, so he would love me, too," she added in a near whisper.

Because he didn't know what to say to that, Sam kept quiet, watching the emotions play across her face. Fighting a totally inappropriate urge to reach out to her, just to hold her hand—a gesture he knew she would reject instantly.

"You wonder why I'm telling you these things," she said perceptively. "You think I'm making a play for your sympathy—and maybe you're right. I'm trying to make you understand how badly I want to see my mother. It's something I've wanted all my life."

"I can understand that. Hell, I'd feel the same way. But what if—"

"What if I get there and find out she really *is* crazy?" Jessica supplied when he hesitated.

He nodded, relieved that she had spelled it out so he didn't have to.

She shrugged and spoke in a tone that was obviously intended to sound nonchalant, but wasn't quite. "I'm aware that's a possibility. I can deal with it. I just have to know for certain."

"And how will you know for certain? Sometimes people who aren't…well, quite right can sound pretty persuasive."

"I'll know," Jessica repeated stubbornly. "Once I see her, talk to her, look into her eyes—I'll know. Besides, I have letters from her. Very lucid, believable letters. I think she's been kept locked up by my father for all these years just because she was an inconvenience to him."

"That's a pretty strong charge. And an unlikely one," he added gently. "Inconvenient relatives aren't just locked away these days without cause."

"Now *you're* the one who is being naive. With enough money, any nuisance can be made to disappear."

He didn't like being called naive. But he couldn't really disagree with her cynicism, either. Money did have a way of making unpleasant situations go away, he thought wryly. Wasn't that the very reason that Walter Parks was so confident he would serve little, if any, time for whatever crimes he'd been accused of?

But the Parks money didn't explain all of Jessica's behavior that Sam had observed during the past few weeks. "What about Derek Ross?"

She blinked a couple of times, but recovered quickly. "What about him?"

He figured if Jessica was willing to lay her cards on the table he should reciprocate—to a point. Besides, he needed to hear her side of the story before he formed his opinions. "Your father said Ross was once involved with your mother and now he's resurfaced to seek revenge against your family. He said Ross is dangerous, and he worries that he's using you in whatever scheme he's hatching."

"So that's the story Dad will use in the courtroom," Jessica murmured. "That Derek is demented and obsessed with revenge, so his testimony can't be trusted."

Sam lifted an eyebrow. "Ross is going to testify against your father?"

"So I'm told."

"Concerning the embezzlement charges?"

Jessica held his gaze steadily. "Concerning the murder charges."

"You think your father is guilty of killing his business partner twenty-five years ago?"

She framed her reply with care. "I think my father is capable of just about anything, Mr. Fields. And if you think that's paranoia, then you really don't know him very well."

The good news was that Sam Fields, if that was his real name, hadn't yet tried to haul her back to San Francisco.

The bad news was that he was there at all.

Jessica had a nagging suspicion that she was wasting her breath trying to make him understand why this trip was so very important to her. He probably couldn't care less as long as he got paid for following her around.

But still, he was listening. Even if he was doing so only to relieve the boredom of sitting in an airport, as long as they were talking she had a chance of getting through to him. And he had admitted that he knew what it was like to be unfairly criticized by a parent, which gave them a small point of reference—assuming he'd told the truth, of course.

"Well, Mr. Fields?" she prodded when he didn't immediately respond to her comment. "Don't you believe my father is capable of anything? Or would admitting it make you equally as bad, since you're willing to take his money?"

Okay, maybe digging at him wasn't the best way to bring him over to her side, she thought with a slight wince. Sometimes words just seemed to leap straight from her mind to her mouth without much interference in between, a trait that had gotten her in trouble too many times to count.

His eyes narrowed, and she had the sudden feeling that the temperature in the room had just risen a couple of degrees. She remembered those angry green flames in his eyes; she seemed to have a knack for igniting them.

For a moment, she thought he would tell her again that he wasn't for sale. But maybe he realized, as she did, that it was going to take more than words to convince her.

"Tell me what your mother said in her letters. And what Derek Ross has been telling you when you've met with him during the past few weeks," he ordered instead of responding to her question about her father.

"My mother told me that my father has kept her committed in Switzerland against her will."

"That's what you would expect her to say, whether she needed to be there or not."

"Perhaps. But she swears she was never diagnosed with the problems he claims. My father tells everyone that she was bipolar to the point of dysfunction, an alcoholic, suicidally depressed, completely out of control. He considered her a danger to herself and to her children, and that—combined with the lack of privacy for wealthy, prominent families in California—was why he sent her to Switzerland. He said that no medication has been effective for her in the long term and that she has never been deemed ready for release. According to Dad, she's had the best doctors available, but her condition is incurable."

"And Derek Ross?"

"Also according to my father, Derek is an example of how seriously disturbed my mother was. Derek is several years younger than my mother—he was barely twenty-two when he had an affair with her. Dad's explanation is that she found an equally troubled young man and seduced him by convincing him that she was being emotionally abused by her cold, evil husband. I don't think Dad knew about Derek when he sent Mother away, but he found out recently—when Derek surfaced along with rumors that he knows something incriminating about Dad's old partner's death."

Sam was beginning to look impatient. "All you're telling me is your father's side of the story. What have your mother and Ross told you?"

"Exactly what my father claims they would say," she replied flatly. "Mother admits she had problems with alcohol and depression, but she said she was never a danger to anyone, especially the children she loved. Derek told me that he met her when he was only twenty-two and fell desperately in love with her. Though he spared me the details, I got the impression the affair was very brief—maybe little more than a one-night stand. But he swears she was entirely sane, and that my father sent her away because she was a danger to him."

"What kind of danger?"

Jessica drew a deep breath. "Derek claims to have watched my father dispose of Jeremy Carlton's body. He said he told my mother about it just before she was sent away. She already had her suspicions, since she was on the yacht the night Carlton disappeared, and she heard my father and Carlton arguing violently."

Sam's expression held the skepticism Jessica had expected. "Why didn't Ross go to the police?"

"He was twenty-two. My father was already a very powerful man. After my mother disappeared, Derek was afraid the same thing would happen to him. He wasn't told what had happened to her, only that she was sent away. He didn't even know if she was still alive. He didn't think anyone would believe his story, especially if they found out he'd slept with Walter Parks's notoriously unstable wife. He left town and changed his name, living with his guilt and his memories until earlier this year, when Jeremy's sons—really my father's illegitimate children from his affair with Jeremy's wife—tracked him down while they were investigating their father's twenty-five-year-old death.

"He married not long after he left town," she added. "He had a daughter he raised alone after his wife died. He didn't want to risk the life he had built for her until his conscience gave him no other choice."

"And he told you all of this because…?"

"Why would he lie?"

"Maybe because he really is unbalanced. Face it, Jessica, it isn't exactly normal for a twenty-two-year-old man who supposedly witnessed a murder to simply skip town and change his name."

"Once again—he didn't think anyone would believe him. And he was afraid my father would hire someone to get rid of him."

"So he says. Maybe he's resurfaced for other reasons."

"Such as—?"

"Revenge. Money. If the Carltons are really out to hang your father in revenge for their father's murder and their mother's untimely death, they could have offered him a hefty bribe in return for his testimony."

Jessica shook her head. "He isn't like that."

In her opinion, Derek Ross was a nice guy—though admittedly somewhat weak to have given in to fear rather than do the right thing. The fact that he had married very quickly after he had moved away indicated that his emotions had been volatile twenty-five years ago. Still, he adored his daughter and wanted now to make amends with his past.

He fully supported Jessica in her quest to bring her mother home, though he'd said there was little he could do to help her, since he had to stay in San Francisco until the upcoming hearings. Even after meeting with him several times, Jessica had felt there were things he wasn't telling her, but still she instinctively trusted him—to a point. Maybe revenge was a part of his motive in testifying, but she didn't believe he was after money.

It annoyed her that Sam's gaze seemed to have become a bit pitying—as if he had no doubt that she was being too trusting. She lifted her chin defiantly. "I know what I'm doing, Mr. Fields. I'm going to see my mother. And there's nothing you can do to stop me."

He studied her face for so long that it was all she could do not to squirm beneath his scrutiny. She managed to hold her ground, keeping her eyes locked with his.

"Your father's going to try to stop you," he said after what felt like an eternity.

"Yes." She had no doubt of that.

Sam propped his elbows on the table and tented his fingers in front of his face, still studying her over them. "According to him, the Carltons are an embittered family who have had it in for him for some time. He swore to me that he's been set up and that his lawyers will make that very clear in court. He doesn't expect the prosecutors to have enough solid evidence to go to trial."

"Yes, that's what he's told me, as well," she replied steadily. "I hope he can prove his innocence in Jeremy Carlton's death. The thought that my father might have murdered someone is hardly comforting. Maybe Derek was wrong about what he thought he saw. After all, it was nighttime—and he'd been drinking—and he was very young."

She had looked for every hole in Derek Ross's story since she had first heard it. As many problems as she'd had with her father over the years, she didn't want to believe he was capable of murder.

"Whatever happened with Jeremy Carlton, I have to know for certain whether my father had my mother locked away because she was an inconvenience to him. I have to know if he's been telling the truth about her mental state—if he has, I want to find out what can be done to help her now."

Sam nodded. "That sounds reasonable."

She held her breath, waiting for him to enlighten her about what his next step would be. Was it too much to hope that he would concede her right to live her own life and go back to San Francisco without her?

She was taken completely aback when he said simply, "I'll go with you."

Jessica stared at Sam as if she couldn't quite believe she'd heard him correctly. "You'll do *what?*"

He lifted one shoulder in a slight shrug. "I'll go with you," he repeated. "I've already got tickets on your flights. This way I can be sure you're safe while you do whatever you feel you need to do."

"No." She had started shaking her head even before he finished speaking. "You can't go with me."

He merely lifted an eyebrow as an invitation for her to explain her reasons for refusing his company.

"I don't know you," she said bluntly. "I don't trust you. I don't want you to go to Switzerland with me."

He didn't take offense at her objections, so his tone was mild when he replied, "I won't interfere with your plans, unless I believe you're in danger."

"You're offering to serve as my bodyguard."

"I already am your bodyguard," he reminded her with a faint smile. "I have been for a while. Your father believes it's necessary, and I tend to agree with him— at least for the duration of this journey."

It was obvious that she'd been trying her best to be

calm and persuasive during their talk, but now her face took on that mulish expression he had come to recognize so well. "I don't want a bodyguard. I don't want you."

It irritated him to realize that he was suddenly wondering what it would take to make her want him, and not as a bodyguard. Especially since he had wanted her from the first time he'd seen her. Which didn't mean he intended to do anything about it, of course.

An involvement with Jessica Parks—even if he managed to talk her into it—was a recipe for disaster if he'd ever seen one. And Sam Fields was all about self-preservation these days—or at least, that was what he'd been trying so hard to believe.

"You have a choice," he said, pushing those irrelevant thoughts to the back of his mind. "You can accept my services, or you can resign yourself to having me follow you around the way I have been. Without your consent."

"You're determined to go to Switzerland?"

He patted the chest pocket of the leather bomber jacket he'd worn over a white oxford cloth shirt and faded jeans—the clothes he'd had on when he'd received Ed's call that morning. "I have my ticket right here. I don't intend to waste it."

Sam had never been particularly drawn to pouty women, but he had to admit that the way Jessica's full lower lip protruded slightly with her discontented frown made something tighten in his abdomen. A man couldn't help but look at that lip and wonder how it would taste, he reasoned. There was no need to read any more than that into it.

"I suppose I don't really have a choice at all," she murmured after a while. "You've already messed everything up, anyway, by calling my father."

"There's not a lot he can do to interfere from a jail cell," he pointed out, though he couldn't help remembering Walter's comment that he would do what he could from his end to keep Jessica from seeing her mother.

Jessica's expression turned wry. "I wouldn't have put it past my father to have arranged this snowstorm."

He couldn't help smiling faintly. "I think that might be giving him a bit too much credit."

She pushed her tumbled blond hair out of her face and murmured wearily, "When it comes to my father, it never pays to underestimate him. Or to anger him," she added in what might have been a subtle warning.

Damned if he would let Jessica's paranoia get to him. He'd made his decision to protect her during this pilgrimage she had planned for so long, and he would follow through—whether Walter Parks approved or not.

He decided it was best not to question his reasons too closely. Suffice it to say, he decided, when Sam Fields took a job, he saw it through to the end.

The morning dawned cold but sunny. As soon as it was light, the airport crews began to work on the runways, clearing them for takeoffs and landings. A general air of expectancy ran through the restless crowd in the airport terminals, and everyone began to prepare for departure.

Jessica tried to freshen up in the crowded ladies'

room, jostling for space in front of the mirrors so she could wash her face and comb her hair. She applied just enough makeup to keep her from looking pale and wan from tension and lack of sleep. Relieved that her clothes were still relatively fresh-looking, she tucked her tote bag beneath her arm, draped her black down coat over one arm and left the rest room.

Sam waited practically in the doorway, his arms folded across his chest and his booted feet crossed as if he was prepared to wait all day if necessary. He must have made short work of his own rest room visit, she thought with a touch of resentment. He looked as though he hadn't quite trusted her not to try to slip away from him—though she couldn't imagine where he thought she'd have gone.

Even though she knew she was wasting her breath, she tried one more time to reason with him. "Surely you have something better to do than go with me to Switzerland."

He shrugged, the smile in his eyes telling her that he knew exactly what she was trying to do. "I don't have any other plans. You're my only client at the moment."

"I am not your client."

He only smiled and motioned toward the gate where their plane was scheduled to depart. "We'd better get started on the security checks again. I've heard we could be boarding within the hour."

She didn't know how he accomplished it, but Sam managed to get the seat next to hers on the plane to Zurich. Now that he wasn't trying to hide from her anymore, he seemed to find it amusing to stay right at her side, making it difficult for her to ignore him. She tried, anyway, responding to his comments in monosyllables, avoiding his eyes as much as possible.

As soon as she was in her seat, she buckled the belt and pointedly buried her face in her book again. Surely even this guy could take that hint.

She should have known better.

"Are you going to ignore me all the way to Switzerland?" His voice was a low growl in her left ear.

She didn't look up from her book. "I'm going to try."

He chuckled. "Not very friendly of you."

"One doesn't have to be particularly friendly to the hired help."

She'd hoped to annoy him enough that he would back off. Instead, he merely laughed again.

She really wished he would quit doing that. Something about his rumbly laughter did funny things to her insides—and she did *not* want to be attracted to this man.

He still worked for her father, despite his promise to see her safely to her mother, and she would do well to keep that thought in the front of her mind. She could not trust her father—nor could she trust anyone who worked for him.

The engines began to rev, filling the cockpit with noise and the curious tension that always accompanies takeoff. Jessica clutched the armrests, preparing herself to leave the safety of the ground. She hoped the ground crew had done their job well so that the plane wouldn't skid off the runway. She hoped there was no ice on the wings, or wherever else ice built up and caused planes to crash.

"Nervous flyer?"

She could lie about it, but since she was clinging to the armrests for dear life, she doubted he would believe her. "Yes."

"Want to hold my hand?"

She curled her fingers more tightly around the armrest. "No."

"The offer stands if you change your mind."

"That's very kind of you." She tried to infuse her tone with sarcasm, even though her voice wasn't as steady as she would have liked.

"Just doing my job, ma'am."

It was obviously a mocking referral to her crack about the "hired help." Scowling down at her lap, she told herself she was quickly learning to hate this guy. But as the plane shot down the runway, it was all she could do not to reach for his hand.

Chapter Six

In preparation for the long flight to Zurich, Sam had bought a couple of paperbacks at an airport newsstand. Jessica had made it clear that she wasn't in the mood to talk, so he pulled out one of the books and settled in to wait. He wouldn't be the guy who bugged her on this flight, he vowed, but he'd bet before they landed she would be ready for conversation.

He stifled a smile when she pulled out an MP3 player half an hour into the trip and slipped the headphones rather defiantly over her ears. Oh, yeah, the silence was getting to her. Without glancing at her, he turned a page in his book, which would have been good enough to hold his attention had Jessica not been sitting so temptingly close to him.

Another twenty minutes passed before he heard her

make a sound that might have been a quick, muffled chuckle. He glanced in her direction, lifting his eyebrows in question. "Did you say something?"

She made a little face, her tone gruff when she replied, "I'm just listening to my theme song."

Without asking for permission, he reached over and removed her headphones.

"Hey," she protested, reaching for them, but he evaded her hand, slipping the earpieces into place so that he could hear the song that had amused her.

Because he spent a lot of time in his car and usually had the radio on while he drove, he recognized the song immediately. Matchbox Twenty's "Unwell." The singer insisted he wasn't crazy, just a little "impaired."

Sam didn't find the song as wryly funny as Jessica had. He tugged the earpieces away and handed them back to her. "You aren't crazy."

"Trying to convince me or yourself?" She turned off the player and stuffed it back into her tote bag. "Has anyone ever told you that you're entirely too pushy?"

"Once or twice." But he was still thinking about her so-called "theme song." "Why do you keep making cracks about being crazy?"

Looking out the window beside her, she shrugged. "That's what everyone says."

"Who's everyone? Your family? Your friends? Your doctors?"

She gave him a look then. "I haven't seen a doctor since I was thirteen. That one diagnosed me as angry and rebellious, but not seriously disturbed. I think my father was hoping the shrink would recommend I be put away—it would have made life so much easier for him."

"According to you, he didn't wait for such advice before having your mother locked away."

"My mother had no one to fight for her. Her drinking and depression had isolated everyone who had once cared for her. I had Brenda."

"Brenda?"

"Our housekeeper. She said all along there was nothing wrong with me that love wouldn't cure. She would have fought anyone who tried to lock me up, and Dad knew it. Because he valued her housekeeping and child-care skills too much to risk losing her, he turned me over to her and pretty much ignored me until he found out when I was eighteen that I had been corresponding with my mother. You can bet he got involved with my life again then."

"How did you get into contact with your mother?"

"I broke into his office when he was away one weekend and found the address of the asylum where he'd placed her. He had it well hidden, but I was persistent. When my father found out about it, I told him I'd found it while I was rummaging through his office to steal money for cigarettes. I didn't smoke—never could stand the smell—but I didn't think he needed to know that."

"You got a kick out of defying your father, huh?"

"As often as possible." She looked out the window again. "I guess I believed then that negative attention was better than no attention at all. I lied, I stole, I ran away, I did anything I could to get my father just to see me."

Sam found that quiet statement especially poignant. He pictured Jessica as a lonely little girl, fantasizing about the mother she had never known, striving for attention from the father who saw her only as an uncomfortable reminder of the wife he had sent away. A little girl who felt loved only by a paid housekeeper, and who would rather be punished than ignored.

He scowled when he realized he was doing it again—letting sympathy interfere with the objectivity he was trying so hard to maintain.

As if she had suddenly realized that she was getting too chatty with someone she had already proclaimed she didn't trust, Jessica crossed her arms and leaned her head against the back of her slightly reclined seat. "I'm tired. I'm going to take a nap."

"Good idea. We've got a long trip ahead of us."

She didn't respond.

Sam leaned back against his own headrest, his face turned so that he could look at her. She really was beautiful. She had the most perfect skin. Like…he hated thinking in clichés, but porcelain was the best comparison he could come up with. Except that porcelain was cold and hard. He would bet Jessica's skin was warm, and very, very soft.

"You're looking at me," she complained without opening her eyes.

"Yes."

"Stop it."

"If you insist." He turned his head forward and closed his eyes. A nap didn't sound like such a bad idea to him, either.

* * *

Jessica returned to full consciousness in small steps. She became aware first of the steady hum of jet engines, and then the sounds of other passengers talking. The overhead vent blew a soft rush of cool air directly onto her right cheek. Her left cheek was comfortably cradled against…

Abruptly opening her eyes, she straightened so quickly she nearly threw herself against the window. She couldn't believe she had been sleeping with her cheek on Sam's shoulder. Nor did she believe that she had put herself there. She glared at him.

Flexing his right arm, he gave her a suspiciously innocent smile in return. "Nice nap?"

"I was sleeping just fine in my own seat."

"I was afraid your neck would get stiff. You're a pretty heavy sleeper, aren't you?"

"Only when I'm exhausted." She glanced at her watch. She'd been asleep a little more than an hour, which meant a good five hours remained of this flight. There was nothing of interest to look at through the window, and she was tired of her book. The in-flight movie was one she had seen and didn't particularly like.

She squirmed restlessly in her seat. As much as she told herself to be patient, she was still anxious to reach the conclusion of this seemingly endless journey.

"Would you like to stretch your legs?"

"I'm fine," she answered shortly. "Just bored."

"Want to talk?"

She sighed. "That's all I've done since you showed up in the airport. I've told you just about everything there is to know about me."

"Oh, I doubt that."

She tilted her chin to look at him. "Maybe I should ask *you* some questions."

"What do you want to know?"

For someone who had shown no compunction at butting his nose into her business, he seemed awfully wary about revealing anything about himself. "Is Sam Fields really your name?"

"Of course it's my name."

"How did you hook up with my father?"

"I've done a couple of jobs for him in the past. Security stuff. Background checks. Information on an employee who was stealing from one of the jewelry stores."

"So he figured he could count on you to spy on his daughter."

Sam sighed. "To watch out for his daughter," he corrected. "It made sense to me at the time. Seemed natural that with him in jail and your siblings somewhat scattered, he would worry about your safety. Especially since you've been targeted before by someone hoping to grab a chunk of his fortune."

Jessica scowled. Sam Fields knew entirely too much about her. "He told you I was kidnapped?"

"Yes." A new note of gentleness softened Sam's deep voice now. "He said it was a terrifying ordeal for you."

She made sure there was no emotion at all in her own voice. "Yes. It was."

"For your father, too. He admitted to me that he's been overprotective since. He implied that he's recently heard rumors that he or his family could be in danger again with everything in such a turmoil because of his arrest."

Jessica locked her fingers in her lap so tightly that her knuckles ached. Voicing her suspicions about that kidnapping would serve no purpose other than to reinforce Sam's belief that she was paranoid about her father.

"Considering that history, and your unwillingness to take precautions on your own behalf, it seemed only reasonable to me to serve as your bodyguard for a few weeks. Just until after the hearing."

"I'm sure he paid you very well for your services."

She knew it annoyed him whenever she mentioned money, but she couldn't resist the occasional dig. Besides, it seemed like a good idea to remind herself every once in a while that the sympathy and concern Sam displayed toward her had been bought and paid for.

"You said you called my father when you figured out my travel plans yesterday," she said when he refused to respond to her comment. "What did he say when you talked to him?"

"I consider my communications with my client to be privileged information."

Narrowing her eyes at him, she noted the irritated slant to his nicely shaped mouth. She figured he was paying her back for referring again to his status as her father's employee. "You had no right to discuss my private affairs with anyone else, including my father."

"I was just doing my job, ma'am."

Now she was the one getting irritated again. "Would you please just tell me what he said?" she asked testily.

After a moment during which he seemed to conduct a brief mental debate, Sam shrugged, the gesture making his shoulder brush against hers. "First he asked me to try to stop you."

That admission took her mind off her too vivid awareness of their brief physical contact. "And just how did he think you were going to do that?"

"I don't know. I told him it was too late for that, anyway."

Trying to rein in her temper, she asked, "What did he say then?"

"He told me to follow you. Keep you safe while he…"

"While he did what?" she asked when he hesitated.

"While he did what he could from there to prevent you from seeing your mother."

Jessica's fists clenched more tightly in her lap. "Damn him. Does he really think he can stop me?"

"I don't know how he intended to accomplish it now that you're already on your way. He just asked me to guard you."

She'd had about all she could take of Sam telling her that her father only wanted what was best for her. "Maybe it makes you feel better to believe it, Mr. Fields, but you're wasting your breath trying to convince me that my father only cares about my safety."

"Would you stop calling me 'Mr. Fields'? My name is Sam. And would your father really go to the trouble of hiring me if he wasn't concerned about your safety?"

"To watch me. Not to watch over me. He wants to know where I am and what I'm doing at all times so he can keep me from finding out the truth about my mother. And maybe the truth about him, as well."

"And what do you think you're going to find?"

She could hear no inflection at all in his voice. If he was skeptical, he hid it well, but he wasn't making an effort to assure her that he believed her, either.

"I think he split up our family to protect his own neck, and I think he's trying to do the same thing now. And I think—I think there's a very good chance that he's guilty of everything with which he has been charged. Including murder."

Sam was certainly having his own doubts about Walter's innocence, or lack thereof. It was those mounting questions that had him second-guessing his particular role in this family melodrama. "You think you're going to find all those answers in Switzerland?"

"Yes," Jessica replied with a rather defiant lift of her chin. "I do think I will. Derek said my mother knows the truth about my father."

"Then why hasn't she come forward before? Why hasn't she tried to get back to the States—and to her children?"

Jessica bit her lip. "I don't know. Derek implied there was something holding Mother in Switzerland. I think he started to tell me what it was, but then he stopped himself and told me that perhaps it would be best if I heard it from Mother. Maybe he was worried about my safety—or maybe he was concerned that I would let something slip and it would get back to my father."

"And what do *you* think is holding her there?" He was trying very hard not to form any judgments, but Jessica's story did seem to get more convoluted each time she added a few details.

"I don't know," she repeated, and the look she gave him told him she knew he was having his doubts about Derek Ross's veracity—and possibly her own. "I'll find out when I talk to her."

He stayed quiet for a while, thinking about the things she had said.

Jessica broke the silence, sounding almost reluctant to ask, "Do you think there's really anything my father can do from jail to stop me from seeing my mother?"

"As you've pointed out several times now, enough money can make a lot of things happen. But he hasn't had much time to make arrangements, and surely he's somewhat restricted by his current circumstances."

"If it hadn't been for that snowstorm, I would be there now," Jessica fretted. "Now he's had all this extra time to make trouble."

"I doubt that there was anything he could do—but if he has made trouble, I'll help you see your mother."

Her blue eyes were round with surprise when she turned her head to look at him. "You will?"

"Yes." Now that he'd committed himself, he would follow through.

She blinked, and he couldn't help noticing how long and silky her eyelashes were. Surprisingly dark for a blonde, and she didn't appear to be wearing much makeup. A little eye shadow, maybe. He suspected she'd put on a touch of blusher to hide the pallor her near sleepless night had left behind. But her mouth was unpainted, its soft curves naturally rosy and tempting.

Her voice pulled him out of his mental inventory of her very attractive features. "My father won't like that."

"Too bad. The only thing I agreed to do for your father was to keep you safe."

"If you do anything to cross him, he'll fire you. You'll be lucky to be paid for anything you've already done for him. Not only that, he would use whatever influence he has left to make sure you never get any other assignments. My father is a dangerous man when he's crossed, Sam."

At least she had used his first name that time. The satisfaction he felt at hearing it on her lips was probably stronger than it should have been. "I'm not afraid of your father."

He expected a melodramatically clichéd response— something along the lines of him being a fool. He was taken aback when her eyes filled, and she whispered, "I am."

Now *he* was the one thinking in clichés as he stared into her eyes. Brilliant blue skies seen through a wash of spring rain. Shimmering blue pools. And, oh, hell, he was sinking fast. "Jessica…"

Her chin lifted, her shoulders squared, and she swiped a hand against her cheeks to erase any trace of tears. Her movements were jerky when she unsnapped her seat belt and stood.

"Excuse me," she said, looking pointedly at his legs. He swung them to one side so she could step past him, and then he watched her as she walked with measured, rapid steps toward the nearest lavatory.

He wasn't the only man watching her, of course,

he noted—but he was the one who would be making the remainder of this journey with her, he reminded himself.

Jessica was furious with herself for giving in to that moment of weakness in front of Sam. She blamed stress, weariness, uncertainty—she blamed herself for once again looking foolish and unstable in front of him.

After splashing water on her face and stalling as long as she could by tying up the lavatory for too long, she returned to her seat with her head high.

"I wasn't crying," she said as she snapped her seat belt. "I'm just a little tense."

"You have every right to be."

"And don't humor me."

"I wouldn't dream of it."

Pulling her book out of her tote bag, she buried her face in it. There were other questions she would have liked to ask him—quite a few more, actually—but she thought she had better shut up for a while now. Before she made an even bigger fool of herself.

Sam gave Jessica plenty of time to collect herself before he tried to engage her in conversation again. They both read for a while, and he dozed, though he didn't think she was able to sleep. A meal was served by the rather bored-looking attendants. Sam ate most of his, but he noticed that Jessica only played with her own food.

"It really isn't that bad."

She looked down at her plate as if she wasn't even sure what she had been served. "No, the food's fine."

"You should try to eat. You don't want to be light-headed by the time we finally arrive in Zurich."

"I'm not very hungry."

"Suit yourself," he said, and turned his attention back to his dessert.

He noticed out of the corner of his eye that she lifted a few bites of food to her mouth then, more an automatic gesture than with any evidence of enjoyment. Satisfied that some of the color was coming back into her face, he finished his own meal, drained his glass of soda, then nodded for the attendant to take his used dishes.

The attendant lingered to flirt for a few minutes, and Sam responded in kind. He figured she was trying to make the routine flight pass more quickly, and he was perfectly willing to share a few laughs toward that end. It wasn't as if Jessica seemed to even notice his presence, so deeply lost was she in her thoughts.

After a couple of minutes, Jessica thrust her plate toward the attendant. "You can take these, too," she said a bit gruffly. "I'm finished with them."

Sam reached out quickly to pluck off the wrapped cookies Jessica had left on the plate.

The attendant smiled at him. "Saving them for a sweet attack later?"

"Something like that," he replied with a smile, though he intended to make sure Jessica ate them later. She would probably need a sugar boost before this trip was over.

"Friendly sort, isn't she?" Jessica muttered when the attendant moved on to chat with another passenger.

"She seems nice."

"Mmph."

He wasn't sure what that muttered syllable meant, but she didn't sound overly impressed with the chatty attendant. Had the circumstances been different, he might have thought she was a bit jealous of the woman's flirting with him. But Jessica didn't even want him on this trip; she certainly didn't want his full attention along the way. More likely her strained nerves were just making her overly sensitive to chatter from other people when she was trying to concentrate on her own problems.

Shortly after the remains of the meal were cleared away, Jessica reached down to her feet and pulled her bulging red tote bag into her lap. Sam was always fascinated when she dug into that bag; she seemed to carry a little bit of everything in it. This time she drew out a green leather-bound spiral journal, set it in her lap, then started digging again.

Whatever else she was looking for seemed to be eluding her. He heard her mutter a curse as she sorted through the bag's contents.

"Lose something?"

"I know I have several pens in this bag, but I can't find one."

Sam had stashed his battered leather jacket beneath his seat. He leaned over to reach into it, then offered her the pen he always carried in his inside pocket. "Use this one."

Setting her tote bag aside, she accepted it. "Thanks. I just want to write a note to myself before I forget."

She studied the white-tipped black rollerball pen for a moment. "Mont Blanc?"

"It's the only gift my ex-wife ever gave me that I kept for sentimental reasons—I used it to sign my divorce papers."

"That's pretty bitter," she said, opening her notebook.

"Not bitter—just slightly sour."

"Were you married long?" she asked, keeping her eyes on her scribbling.

"Thankfully, no."

"How long have you been divorced?"

"Two years."

He figured he owed her a few personal details, considering he'd rummaged through her underwear. Walter hadn't said what suspicious items, exactly, he'd wanted Sam to look for, but he had suggested that Sam would find stolen items and maybe worse. Sam had assumed he meant drugs.

Though he'd found none of the latter, except for a few innocuous prescription and over-the-counter medications, he had found that odd collection of small, tagged items hidden in a dresser drawer. He still wasn't quite sure of their significance, but he couldn't help thinking of Walter's warnings about her shoplifting predilection. The compulsion seemed to intensify under stress, Walter said, and Jessica herself claimed she'd been under a lot of stress lately.

He had to admit that Jessica made him question everything Walter had told him. She seemed to have good reason to resent her father's interference in her life. And other than being a bit scatterbrained—partially explained by the facts that she was an artist and totally obsessed with getting to her mother before Walter stopped her—Sam had seen no indication that Jessica had serious problems.

"So you're the type who writes memos to herself, hmm?"

Still writing, she nodded. "I tend to forget things if I don't jot them down."

"Ever considered getting a PDA? They have calendars and notepads and alarm clocks and all sorts of other useful features for people who tend to be forgetful. I carry a small one myself, in the same jacket pocket with my pen."

"I've been given three of them for various occasions. I managed to lose one, fry the circuits on another, and I never learned how to use the latest one. I'll stick with a purse calendar and a notebook for now. I like to keep things simple."

"Now why do I find that so hard to believe?"

"I can't imagine," she replied, closing her notebook a bit huffily. She slid both the notebook and his pen into her tote bag, her mouth still turned into a slight pout, as if she thought he'd been mocking her.

"Um—my pen?" he reminded her.

Her expression went from annoyed to mortified. Waves of red darkened her cheeks, and she scrambled almost frantically in the bag to retrieve the pen. "I'm so sorry," she said with a dismay that seemed out of proportion for such a minor lapse. "I wasn't paying attention to what I was doing. I really didn't intend to keep it."

Lifting a quizzical eyebrow in her direction, he accepted the pen and slipped it into the pocket of his white cotton shirt. "No problem. I'm the one who was distracting you."

"Still, it was a stupid thing to do."

"Jessica, it's okay," he said firmly, laying a hand over hers, which were now clasped so tightly in her lap it looked painful. "I do things like that all the time. Everyone does."

The tormented look in her eyes told him she hadn't found his words particularly reassuring. He tightened his hands over hers, and thought he felt them trembling slightly. "It's going to be okay," he repeated, and he was no longer talking about the pen.

Whatever demons Jessica Parks had been battling, she had been fighting them all by herself for entirely too long, in Sam's opinion. It was time for someone to step forward and help her with them.

Although he had never considered himself the unselfishly heroic type—and he would sure as hell bet that Jessica didn't see him that way—it seemed that it had fallen to him to offer his services. Certainly no one else was hurrying to give her a hand.

Chapter Seven

The hand Sam had placed over hers was warm. Gentle. Yet reassuringly strong. Jessica was very nearly tempted to turn her own hand over so that their palms were clasped. She resisted only because she had never been the type to cling to anyone else and she had no intention of starting now, certainly not with this man.

She reached up to push a lock of hair behind her ear as an excuse to draw away from him. Taking the hint, he pulled his hand to his own side of the armrest.

Jessica drew a deep breath. "I think we need to get a few things straight before we land in Switzerland."

"I'm listening."

"I've been doing some thinking during this flight. It's clear that I'm not going to be able to force you to go back to San Francisco and let me finish the rest of this trip on my own."

"Right on that point."

"Let me continue. It would do me no good to fight you or try to run away from you. It would cause delays I can't afford, and bring attention to us that I don't want. It occurred to me at one point that I'm being awfully trusting to take your word that you are who you say you are, and that I really will be safe with you in a foreign country. For all I really know, *you* could be leading me into danger, or planning some stunt to get your hands on my father's money."

He nodded somberly. "I can see where that might occur to you. I realize I'm a stranger to you. I could show you my driver's license, but those can be faked."

"Exactly. So all I have to go on is your word, and my own instincts."

"I can tell you my word is reliable. How are your instincts?"

"To be candid, they haven't been that great in the past. I've trusted some people I shouldn't have, and re- lied on others who let me down."

"Haven't we all," he muttered, and she wondered if he was referring to the ex-wife of whom he had spoken with such rancor. He seemed to shake off a bad mem- ory before asking, "What are your instincts telling you about me?"

"That I can trust you."

He looked a bit surprised. Before he could say any- thing, she held up a finger to silence him and qualified, "To a point."

"And what point is that?"

"I won't try to stop you from tagging along with me to Lausanne—but I want you to keep in mind that this is *my* journey. I didn't hire you as a bodyguard, and I don't want you interfering with my actions 'for my own good.' Nor will I allow you to try to control me on directions from my father. I've spent the past three years planning this trip, and I will not let you—or anyone else—get in my way."

"You sound very stern. I can't help wondering how you would stop me if I *did* try anything. Considering that you're about half my size."

"I don't know exactly what I would do," she answered honestly. "I'm certain only that I will not be stopped this time. Dad can give it his best shot—making trouble, sending people to interfere. Even arranging another fake kidnapping. None of it will work."

"*Another* fake kidnapping?" Sam leaped on that word with a sharpness that made her regret her imprudent tongue.

She shrugged. "I'm just saying it doesn't matter what he tries, he can't stop me from seeing my mother this time."

"Jessica." He leaned very close to her so he could speak too quietly to be overheard by any of their fellow travelers. "Are you telling me that you think your father paid someone to kidnap you eight years ago?"

She kept her own voice steady, despite a jump of nerves she attributed as much to his physical closeness as his question. "It took me a long time—years—to come to that conclusion, but yes, I think that's exactly what he did."

"What evidence do you have to support that claim?"

She lifted her eyebrows. "Were you by any chance a lawyer before you went into your current line of work?"

"I was a cop."

Interesting. "Yet you're working for a man who's in prison on murder and embezzlement charges?"

He had the grace to look uncomfortable. "I told you, I've worked for him before. He has always been considered an upstanding member of the business community. A bit ruthless, of course, but that's true of most of the powerful tycoons. He never asked me to do anything to cross my own ethical boundaries."

Jessica couldn't help wondering whether Sam's 'ethical boundaries' came anywhere close to her own.

"Anyway, why do you think he arranged to have you kidnapped?"

"The timing, for one thing. I had only recently discovered my mother's whereabouts, and I had started a secret correspondence with her through a post-office box I rented near my school. I took all my graduation money and what little I'd been able to earn by working in one of the jewelry stores, and I bought a ticket to Switzerland. My father confronted me with the letters I had received from my mother only a few days after I was returned by the kidnappers."

"Maybe he came across the letters in the process of looking for clues to your kidnappers. Maybe he thought they were connected in some way to your disappearance."

"He said he got a ransom call the same night I was snatched on my way to the airport. He told me he found the letters while searching my wardrobe to find out what

I was wearing so he could give a description to the police if necessary. I don't think that was the truth. I think he'd found out about my travel plans and arranged to interfere in a way that would keep me from going and make sure I would be too frightened to try again."

"He told me you weren't injured during your ordeal."

"Not physically. But I was locked in a very small, very dim room for almost two weeks. I had no human contact, except for a man who delivered food and water without speaking to me. I was given a couple of old magazines and a battery-powered radio to help me pass the time, but the minutes crept by so slowly I honestly thought I would die in there—if my kidnappers didn't kill me first."

"Your kidnappers never threatened you? Never asked any questions about your family?"

"They never spoke to me," she repeated. "When I asked questions, I was ignored. Just as they ignored me when I cried and…and when I begged to go home," she admitted. She hated to remember the emotional state she had been reduced to at the end of the ordeal.

He didn't seem to notice the slight break in her voice. "How were you released?"

She actually appreciated that he didn't offer any sympathy. His matter-of-fact questioning, whether intentional or not, helped her keep her voice steady. "I was blindfolded, and I was led outside to a car. There were two men. The only one who spoke to me said something like, 'You're going home, kid.' I thought they might be taking me someplace to kill me and dispose of my body.

"To be honest," she added in a near whisper, "by that

point I didn't really care. Anything was better than spending another day in that room."

"Where were you dropped off?"

"At the front gate of the estate. The man who had spoken to me got out of the car, opened my door, removed my blindfold and told me to get out. As soon as I did, they drove away. I stared after the car for a minute, then turned and ran as fast as I could through the gates."

"The front gates were open?"

"Yes. They aren't usually, but they happened to be then. I burst through the front door crying. Brenda grabbed me in a hug so tight I thought I would break, but it felt wonderful. Then my sister and my brothers hugged me. Emily was crying," she added. "Cade was trying not to."

"And your father?"

"He hugged me, of course. Briefly." She remembered clinging to him when he stopped hugging. He had placed his hands on her shoulders to hold her a few inches away from him then. "He said he was glad I was home safely. And then he reminded me that it never would have happened if I hadn't been so foolish. He said people with our wealth don't have the luxury of heading off alone, without taking certain security precautions."

"In effect, blaming you for what happened to you."

"That was the way I interpreted it."

But Sam's attention was already turning back to the details. "The security cameras at the gates of your father's estate—were they there eight years ago?"

"Yes. They've been in place for as long as I can remember. He updates them every couple of years."

"Were you dropped off within range of those cameras?"

She thought back. "Yes. As I said, we were right at the front gates."

"Which were open."

"Yes."

"The vehicle you were in—did it have a license plate?"

"Yes. I remember thinking I should try to memorize the number as I watched it drive away, but it just seemed like too much effort then."

"Yet the kidnappers were never caught."

"My father said there was no way to track them down."

"Did the police have you give descriptions to an artist? Did they try to help you remember details of the car or the license plate?"

"I never spoke to the police."

She heard the questions in Sam's silence. "My father said he kept the police out of it because the kidnappers said they would kill me if he called them."

"For two weeks?"

She nodded.

"And what about after you were returned safely?"

"He said it was too late to find any leads. And he didn't want the media to find out about it. He said if it became general knowledge that he had been willing to pay a substantial ransom for my return, we would all be targeted by greedy felons."

Sam raised a hand to squeeze the bridge of his nose.

"It all sounded entirely reasonable at the time," she told him. "My father can be very convincing."

"Tell me about it."

She wondered if his disgruntled mutter meant that he had finally begun to question some of the things Walter had said to him.

"As I've said, it was some time later when I began to question whether he might have had some role in the kidnapping. We were raised never to question our father, though Rowan and I did our share of rebelling during our teens. I suppose I did more than my share. And I still felt guilty for being careless and getting kidnapped."

"It wasn't your fault."

She knew now that she had been guilty only of being young, naive and reckless. "I know."

"So after that you stopped trying to get to your mother."

"Yes. I was a mess, emotionally. I couldn't have dealt with the stress of planning another escape. Besides, I had no money. My father made certain of that. He gave me just enough to get by with a few luxuries, but not enough to finance a trip to Switzerland."

"Did you continue your correspondence with her?"

"He stopped that, too. He closed my post-office box and started monitoring my mail at home. I didn't even know she was still in Switzerland until I received another letter from her three years ago. It came to my cottage address, disguised as a credit card solicitation. I don't know how she arranged that—I assume she had some assistance. Since then my mother and I have been secretly writing again. I've heard from her maybe five times in the past three years. She can't risk writing very often."

Sam was quiet for a short while, apparently digesting everything she'd told him to that point. "I have just one more question," he said finally. "For now."

"What?"

"If you've had so much distrust of your father for so long, why do you continue to live on his estate? You're what, twenty-six?"

He probably knew exactly how old she was. Her cheeks burned with resentment when she answered. "I moved out for a while, after I recovered from the kidnapping. I got an apartment in San Francisco a few years ago. My father was opposed to it, but I was working for someone else by then, making enough to pay my rent. I'd been living there only a few months when I was mugged."

"Damn."

"Yeah. That time I *was* hurt. I fought back, you see, instead of just letting him take my purse."

"Not exactly a wise thing to do."

"I was just so angry—maybe I was tired of being a victim. But it was a stupid thing to do. The mugger didn't seem to want to fight me, but I jumped on his back, and he reacted by flinging me off. I fell with one leg under me, and it shattered. It was a while before I could return to work, and by that time I'd lost my job and my apartment. I moved into the cottage with my father's promise that he would stay out of my life, which I took with a grain of salt. While I was recuperating, I started painting. It was my success with my paintings that let me stash away enough money to fund this trip."

He nodded. "So you stayed on the estate to be safe and to save money."

He still didn't seem to understand, exactly, but his summation was close enough. "Right."

Their conversation was interrupted by an announcement that the plane was beginning to descend toward Zurich. Jessica felt her pulse rate speed up in response.

"I've never been out of the States before," she told Sam. "I think I'm a little nervous."

"I'll keep you safe."

She scowled at his automatic response. "I wasn't asking for your help. I was simply making a comment."

His sudden grin made her already accelerated pulse go into overdrive. "Sorry. I accidentally slipped into bodyguard mode for a minute."

She managed somehow to hang on to her stern expression. "Well, stop it."

"Yes, ma'am," he murmured.

She didn't buy his meek expression for a minute. The minute Sam felt it necessary, he would go straight back into what he called "bodyguard mode." While there was some sense of security in knowing that he was there to watch out for her, she was glumly aware that it wasn't helping her in her quest to become a more independent and self-sufficient woman.

Though it was only midafternoon Chicago time, it was nearly 10:00 p.m. in Zurich, and it would be nearly twelve hours before Jessica and Sam would be able to depart for Geneva. The delay in Chicago had really fouled up Jessica's travel plans, turning what should have been an eighteen-hour journey into a three-day ordeal.

"Look at it this way," Sam said when her frustration

and impatience nearly got the best of her. "You wanted an adventure."

"I want to see my mother," she corrected him, and hated the primness of her own voice.

He cocked an eyebrow at her. "And the thought of being in a foreign country, far away from your father, doesn't excite you at all?"

When he put it that way...

She looked around the crowded terminal, letting the exotic mixture of sights and sounds wash over her. She must have heard more than half a dozen languages being spoken just within hearing distance of where she and Sam stood. And, yes, it was a bit exciting for a woman who had been so strictly sheltered and restricted for all of her life.

"Of course," she said. "But it isn't as if there will be time for sight-seeing between now and takeoff tomorrow morning."

"Not sight-seeing, maybe—but how about a little fun?"

"Fun?" She hardly remembered the meaning of the word. "Like what?"

He took her arm. "Let's get checked in to a hotel for the evening, and then we'll see what we can find."

She hesitated, frowning at him.

Sam sighed. "Separate rooms. Large crowds," he added, sweeping an arm around the bustling terminal. "There's no reason to look at me as if I'm taking you to a dark alley to have my nefarious way with you."

She had, after all, agreed to let him accompany her. And she'd said she would trust him—to a point. "Do you think we can find something to eat? I'm starving."

He grinned. "Bet on it."

She really wished he would stop doing that, she thought, mesmerized once again by the high-voltage power of his full smile. She had seen its effect on the flight attendant, and she had no intention of allowing herself to be so easily charmed.

Okay, so Sam Fields was a handy guy to have around at times, Jessica couldn't help admitting, if only to herself.

They were sitting in a cheerfully noisy restaurant-bar with heaping plates of deliciously prepared food in front of them. Sam had found two rooms in a chain hotel near the airport and, after they had quickly showered and changed, had then brought her to this nice place at the edge of the Old Town. He had even managed to procure a tiny table by a window overlooking the River Limmat, so that they had an absolutely stunning view of lights reflecting on purply-black water while they ate.

And he had handled it all in what had sounded to Jessica like flawless German.

Now that she was fairly confident she wouldn't keel over from lack of food, she wanted some answers. "Okay, spill it," she said. "How did you do that?"

He swallowed a mouthful of beef and reached for his wineglass. "Do what?"

"You've been to Zurich before?"

"Yes."

"Really?" It seemed odd for a cop-turned-P.I. to be so well traveled.

He nodded. "You aren't the only one who bought an airline ticket with high school graduation money. I spent two years in Europe—most of the time in Switzerland, Austria and Germany. I waited tables, worked on a couple of dairy farms, schlepped bags at a couple of hotels—whatever I could find to keep me busy and provide a little money."

There were so many interesting things to see around them, but Jessica found her attention focused almost exclusively on her dining companion, who seemed to be the biggest curiosity at the moment. "You speak like a native."

"My mother was German. Dad met her when he was stationed at an air force base there in the midsixties. I spoke both English and German growing up—though mostly English, obviously. My mother was the one who wanted me to come to Europe. She wanted me to meet her family—which I did, though we didn't really hit it off, since all they could do was talk about how much they disliked my father. I didn't stay with them very long before I decided to move on and see other places, to their relief and my mother's disappointment."

"She never came back herself?"

"No. They pretty much disowned her when she married my father against their advice. I think she was hoping my grandfather—who had some money—would like me well enough to forgive her. Unfortunately for her, he much preferred her brother's kids."

"That's very sad, for all of you. But especially for your mother, that she was never reunited with her family."

"You should know what it's like to rebel against a controlling father. And she wasn't completely innocent in the feud. My mother was an angry, bitter, bluntly spoken woman who caused a lot of her own problems."

Jessica knew there were happy families out there somewhere, people who had enjoyed loving, healthy childhoods. She just didn't happen to know any of them. But then, she didn't know that many people—her father had seen to that.

Sam seemed to come to the decision that he was revealing too much about himself. He guided the conversation into a less personal area. "Of course, the German my mother spoke was significantly different from the Swiss German—or Schweizerdeutsch—that's spoken here. There's enough difference that they often show German subtitles on Swiss films shown in Germany."

"You seem to get by very well."

He shrugged. "I've always had an ear for languages."

"That must have been so cool—living and working here, I mean. Did you get homesick?"

"Not particularly. I had a blast here—but then it was time to go home."

"Where you became a cop."

"Eventually, after trying a couple of other things that didn't hold my attention." He shrugged again. "It was what my father wanted. I didn't have any particular aspirations, and I thought it would be a challenge, so I signed up for the police academy when I was twenty-five. Mother was furious, but I reminded her that I'd visited Germany for her. I'd been on the job just over three years when Dad died. That was ten years ago."

Making Sam thirty-eight now, Jessica calculated quickly. She would have guessed him to be several years younger, judging by appearance. "You've had quite a varied background."

"I get bored easily."

She wondered if he had gotten bored with his marriage. Fortunately, that was one impolite question that didn't leap straight from her mind to her mouth.

Her gaze drifted to the window, through which she could see fanciful spires and towers illuminated by bright lights shining up toward the inky skies. She knew there were fascinating things to see on the other side of that glass. Old churches and art galleries, winding, cobbled streets and ornate, gushing fountains.

She wanted to soak in the sights of the snow-topped Alps and Lake Zurich, and to stroll through the shops that lined the famous Bahnhofstrasse. She longed to spend whole days in the galleries admiring and studying the art. But that wasn't why she was here, she reminded herself.

"What do you see out there?" Sam's quiet question cut into her daydreaming.

"Switzerland," she replied with a sigh.

"You aren't like most of the rich young women I've known. Not that I've known that many, of course."

That comment brought her gaze back to him. "What do you mean?"

"You haven't traveled much. You talked about having to save money for this trip. You don't seem to go to a lot of parties and other social affairs."

Which he knew because he had been following her for weeks, she thought with a quick scowl. "I'm not a jet-setter, that's for sure. My father never liked traveling, and the older he's gotten, the less he does it. Needless to say, he didn't let me go off on my own, especially after my rebellious teen years, and my one attempt to escape.

"I don't like big gatherings because I get tired of people pointing and whispering about my family. Wondering when I'm going to flip out like the crazy mother I look just like. And now, of course, speculating about whether my father really killed his business partner."

She reached for her water goblet. "As for the money, my father provided us with a beautiful home, nice clothes and cars, excellent educations and any material possessions we wanted. But the cash flow was carefully controlled, and we were never left in any doubt that it was *his* money. We were totally dependent on him for everything we received."

Sam was quiet for a few moments, and then he asked, "Are you finished with your meal?"

She glanced down at her plate, rather surprised to see that it was almost empty. "Yes."

"It occurs to me that we've spent the entire day talking about your problems with your father—even touched on my family baggage. Why don't we give it a rest for a while?"

He motioned toward the far side of the room, where a wide doorway led into a bustling club. "Want to go listen to some music? Maybe dance a little?"

"Dance?"

"You do dance, don't you?"

"It's been a while, but yes, I dance."

"Then let's go."

There was a brief debate over the check, but Sam insisted on putting the meals on his credit card. "I'm sending the bill to your father's accountant."

"And if they refuse to pay you?"

"Then I'll steal your daddy's limo and sell it to a chop shop," he replied without missing a beat.

"Help me see my mother, and I'll get you the keys to Daddy's limo," she offered recklessly.

He grinned. "Deal."

Chapter Eight

Maybe it was because of the tension she had been under lately, but Sam hadn't seen Jessica smile much. Though he had observed her laughing a couple of times with her tall, blond friend, he had come to think of her as a rather serious young woman, intense, absent-minded, often angry.

Beautiful, but troubled, was the way he had thought of her. Definitely off-limits, even had she not been the daughter of his client. Even had she not been twelve years his junior. Even if he had been looking to get involved with anyone—which he was not.

Sometime during an hour of dancing with her on this spontaneous night in Zurich, he began to rethink quite a few of those earlier impressions.

She had a lovely smile, full and curving, lighting up

a face that was already stunning. Her laugh was a low gurgle that went straight to his abdomen.

She was rather awkward with him at first, skeptical of his reasons for asking her to dance, still not certain just how far she could trust him. The specter of her father had seemed to hover between them all day, but the swirling lights of the dance club soon dispelled that shadow.

Maybe it was the wine. Maybe the setting. Or maybe Jessica really needed a break from her scheming and worrying. Within minutes after joining the crowd, who appeared to be mostly young professionals, on the dance floor, he could see the tension leaving her shoulders. Her eyes were brighter, her cheeks lightly flushed…and she smiled. At him.

He kept his emotions firmly under control as they danced. This evening was for her, he reminded himself. He was doing his job—keeping her safe, fed and entertained.

The music was American pop, peppy and upbeat. Easy to dance to, not particularly challenging to listen to. Just what she needed tonight, he decided. He kept their dancing friendly, platonic, touching her only lightly. He made innocuous small talk, like the near stranger he was to her. He didn't want to remind her of how well he actually knew her, or how he had learned so many very personal details.

Between everything he had been told about her, and the things she had revealed herself, during their flight, there was little about Jessica Parks's background that he didn't know. But he still couldn't say that he knew *her*.

A slower number brought even more people onto the

floor, and Sam held Jessica a bit more tightly. Even as he blamed the crowd, he knew he'd simply been waiting for an excuse to get closer to her.

Their bodies brushed now, and even that light contact was enough to raise his temperature a couple of degrees. She smelled very faintly of flowers. The mere suggestion of scent made him fantasize about burying his face in her soft hair.

The simple black jersey top and slacks she wore had probably been chosen for comfort and carefree packing, but Sam couldn't help admiring the way the fabric skimmed her slender curves and moved with her as she danced. He would have thought she was too fair to wear black, but somehow it worked for her, making her hair look warmer, her eyes bluer.

"You know what's funny?"

Her quiet question brought his mind off her appearance—temporarily, at least. He held her an inch farther away so he could see her face. "What?"

She glanced at the other dancers around them. "It's almost as if we're in a club back home."

He smiled wryly, understanding what she meant. A significant number of the people around them were Americans, travelers here on business or vacation who, like Sam and Jessica, had looked for a comfortable and conveniently located spot to wind down for the evening.

"I should have taken you to one of the more locally patronized places," he mused. "The concierge at the hotel mentioned that there are a lot of new clubs in the fourth and fifth districts around Langstrasse. And I remember a couple of good jazz clubs on Niederdorfstrasse and Oberdorfstrasse. But I was told that the food was good here and the service very quick—"

"Exactly what I needed tonight," she assured him. "I'm really too tired for the more lively clubs."

Someone bumped into him from behind, murmuring an apology in German. Sam responded, but the incident had brought him closer to Jessica again. This time he didn't try to hold her away. She felt so good in his arms— and his willpower had been strained almost to the limit.

A crooning love song began, and their movements slowed to a gentle sway. In a gesture that seemed more wearily content than personal, Jessica rested her head against his shoulder. His pulse leaped, but he thought he did an adequate job of concealing the reaction.

Aware of how easily she could shy away from him— and conscious that only a few hours earlier she had been ready to go for his throat—he laid his cheek very lightly against her hair. Oh, man, it felt as silky as he had imagined.

He hadn't had to struggle with his own body this way since high school. As skittish as Jessica was around him, the first sign that he was reacting quite physically to her nearness would likely send her running.

"I shouldn't be doing this," she murmured, her voice almost too soft to hear above the music.

"Doing what? Dancing?"

"Mmm." The reply was a rather sleepy murmur. "I still don't completely trust you, you know."

Considering the state of his emotions at having her snuggled in his arms, he couldn't say her mistrust was entirely unfounded. "I know."

"I'd intended to keep you at a distance during this trip. I would tolerate your presence, but I would give you no encouragement. I planned to pretty much ignore you."

"Go right ahead," he offered, settling her a bit more snugly against his chest.

Her soft laugh sounded rueful. "I can hardly ignore you while I'm dancing with you."

"I can't tell you how many girls did just that during high school dances."

"Somehow I doubt you've ever been easy to ignore. I spotted you even when you were following me all over San Francisco."

He winced. "You don't have to remind me of that. I really am good at what I do, you know. Very few people have ever spotted me tailing them."

"Yes, well, I'd been expecting my father to have me followed ever since I started planning this trip. I was sure he would know somehow that I was up to something—he always knows. And that he would try to find out what it was so he could interfere. And besides, you're—"

She stopped suddenly, as if she'd almost said something she shouldn't. Which, of course, only made him more curious to know what it was. "I'm what?"

"Noticeable," she said after a moment.

The fact that he liked hearing her admit that—a lot, actually—was merely further evidence that dancing with her wasn't such a good idea.

"Sam?" she asked after a pause, as the slow number was coming to a close.

"Mmm?"

"Could we go back to the hotel now?"

He wouldn't have minded that request so much if he hadn't been fully aware that she was talking about going back to their separate rooms.

"Of course," he said, though it took him a moment to make himself release her. He waited until the very last note of the song had faded away before doing so.

After all, who knew when—or if—he would have the chance to hold her again?

Jessica couldn't believe she had dined and danced with Sam Fields. What had she been thinking?

Well, okay, she knew exactly what she'd been thinking. Sam was a very attractive man. He knew how to be charming and attentive. How to make a woman feel pretty, and flattered by his interest. And she had been so narrowly focused on her quest for answers about her past that she hadn't even dated in almost longer than she could remember.

She was a healthy young woman with a healthy interest in male companionship. Being held in Sam's strong arms had been more than just pleasant. She had been strongly tempted to snuggle close to him and find out exactly how that lean, sexy body felt pressed against her own. He had smelled of soap and a light, spicy aftershave, and she had wanted to bury her face in his neck for a more intimate exploration.

And she barely even knew the guy, she told herself with a bewildered laugh as she crawled into bed, leaving a dim light burning in a far corner of the hotel room. But she knew he danced like a dream. And when he smiled, his deep green eyes crinkled delightfully at the corners. And the shape of his mouth inspired fantasies she shouldn't be having about a man she didn't trust and didn't want to like.

She really *would* be crazy to let herself become infatuated with him, she thought, sinking more deeply into the pillows. Because that thought touched a bit too closely on her darkest fears, she pulled the covers over her head and tried to will herself instantly to sleep.

Sam wasn't particularly surprised to discover the next morning that Jessica had pulled back from him during the night. She had probably spent the hours they were apart reminding herself of his connection to the father she had been struggling so hard to get away from. The pleasant evening they had spent together had been an aberration she surely had no intention of repeating.

At least she looked as though she had gotten some sleep. He studied her face, pleased to see that the signs of strain and exhaustion from the long trip were gone. He still saw hints of tension in her eyes and the set of her shoulders, but he imagined that was the result of his presence and her excitement at being so close to finally seeing her mother.

He was glad she had managed to sleep. He had dozed only fitfully, all too aware that she lay in the room next to him. Remembering how she had felt in his arms. How well they had fit together even with an eight-inch difference in height.

"I don't know about you, but I'm about to get tired of airplane seats," he said as they snapped their seat belts.

"I could go a long time without another takeoff," she agreed, even as the jet's engines began to rev.

He watched her hands tighten in her lap. "Takeoff is the worst part for you?"

"Yes. Once we're in the air, I'm okay. Mostly."

He laid his hand palm up on the armrest. "Some people think it helps to hang on to someone during takeoff."

She glanced at his hand, then away. "I'll be fine."

He grinned and wiggled his fingers. "Just keep in mind that I'm here if you need me."

"Thank you. I'll do that."

"A word of advice? I know you're trying to put me off with that icy, regal tone, but I gotta tell you—it kind of has the opposite effect. Every time you talk to me like that, I just want to kiss you senseless."

She stared at him with widened eyes, looking as though she couldn't believe she had heard him correctly. By the time she recovered, the plane was in the air.

"I suppose you think that was a clever way to take my mind off my anxiety."

"Sure. Okay. If that's what you want to believe."

Eyeing him suspiciously, she pulled out her MP3 player and rather defiantly donned the headphones.

Still chuckling, he leaned back in his seat and looked out the window at the snowy mountains beneath them.

Jessica thought he'd been teasing. And yet, she realized that he had meant exactly what he'd said.

During the four-hour flight from Zurich to Geneva, Jessica might have said half a dozen words to him, and those only in response to questions he asked. She gave every appearance of having forgotten he was there—

which gave him the opportunity to watch her during the trip.

She kept the headphones on most of the time, but he would bet she wasn't really hearing the music. She held one of her books open in her lap, but her eyes didn't track the words and she never turned a page. Rather than looking more excited as they neared their destination, she seemed to grow more tense with each passing mile.

"How are you planning to get to Lausanne?" he asked as the plane began the descent toward the Geneva airport.

"I thought I would take a train."

He considered a moment, then shook his head. "Let's rent a car. It will give us more control."

"But…"

"Don't worry. I'll handle everything."

That made her eyes narrow. "I don't need you to handle anything."

"You might as well use me for something, since I'm here anyway."

She looked quickly away, but not before he spotted a faint wash of pink high on her cheekbones. Had she taken his words as a double entendre? Had she unwillingly thought of another couple of ways to put him to use? Or was that only wishful thinking on his part?

Driving in Switzerland was an adventure, but Sam remembered most of the tricks. Fortunately, the weather was good, and the roads were clear. The other drivers seemed to be sane and sober, for the most part—and being used to San Francisco drivers, he found that a pleasant change, he thought with a wry smile.

It was only a forty-five minute drive from Geneva to Lausanne, and the scenery was spectacular enough to break through Jessica's distraction. "It's so beautiful here," she breathed. "Like paradise."

"I would be more than happy to play Adam to your Eve," he offered, just to get a rise out of her.

He succeeded. She punched his arm.

"Ouch." Laughing, he took his left hand off the steering wheel to massage his right biceps.

"You deserved that."

"Sorry. Couldn't resist."

"Next time…try."

Still grinning, he placed both hands back on the wheel of the tiny rental car.

Jessica's attention had already turned to the scenery again as he carefully approached the city center of Lausanne. "You know what it sort of reminds me of?"

"San Francisco," he answered confidently. "Lausanne is actually referred to sometimes as the San Francisco of Switzerland. The way the city rises from Lac Léman, the steep streets, the vineyards that line the outskirts of the city, the mountains rising beyond—it's very reminiscent of home, isn't it?"

"In some ways. Yet in others, it's very European," she mused, staring wide-eyed at the cars, buses and buildings that she would never see back in California.

Noting the busy streets and filled parking lots, he asked, "Did you make hotel reservations?"

"Yes." She pulled her notebook from her tote bag and read the name of the hotel and its address. "Do you know where that is?"

Her pronunciation made him chuckle, but he managed to disguise it as a cough. "I can find it. Um—you didn't take French in high school, I take it?"

"No. I took Spanish. I'm actually almost fluent in Spanish," she added with a sigh. "Not that it's done me any good on this trip."

"Unlike Zurich, where you hear mostly German, Lausanne is in the French-speaking region. Fortunately, many locals know at least a few words of English."

"I noticed that you spoke French when you rented the car. You sounded pretty good at it. Did you pick that up when you were here before?"

"I took four years of French in high school because someone told me girls are turned on by hearing guys speak in French. I don't suppose it did anything for you when you heard me speaking it…?"

She glared at him.

"Guess not."

"A cop-turned-P.I. who traveled Europe and speaks three languages. I suppose I should be impressed."

"And yet I sense that you're not."

She made a show of yawning delicately behind her hand. "Not particularly."

"Not even if I told you I actually speak four languages with varying degrees of fluency?"

She gave him a suspicious look. "Do you really?"

By way of reply, he informed her—in Spanish—that he hoped there would be a parking garage at the hotel where she'd made reservations, since finding parking places in Lausanne was sometimes difficult.

"Hispanic grandmother?" Jessica asked a bit too politely.

"Hispanic girlfriend."

"Oh, of course."

"Her name was Carmen. She was a grad student whose parents had moved to San Francisco from Mexico City. I dated her for two years after I returned to the States. We had a very amicable split, leaving me with another language, an appreciation for salsa music and a good friend to this day. I'm her oldest son's godfather."

"One thing I can say about you—nothing about you is predictable."

"Good. I can't think of anything worse to be called."

Jessica sighed a bit wistfully. "That's the way most people think of me, you know."

"You? Predictable?" He scoffed, "Yeah, right."

"Surely you followed me around enough to know what a dull life I lead. I paint, have an occasional lunch with a friend, volunteer every Wednesday at a youth center. I rarely do anything daring or impulsive."

"How about this trip?"

"Daring—maybe. Impulsive—hardly. I've been planning it for years."

"Still, I thought you were considered the least predictable member of the Parks family."

"The least stable," she corrected him. "Even in that, I'm fairly predictable. Everyone expects me to have an occasional meltdown or do something rather bizarre— and right on cue, I do."

"Stop being so hard on yourself. You're a talented artist with a promising future. You've made a life and a career for yourself with little support from your family. And you're making a difference in the lives of those kids you work with every Wednesday. So just stop it, okay?"

She stared at him a moment, then said, "I'm not sure if you're complimenting me or yelling at me."

He turned the car into the convenient parking garage of the hotel. "Both."

"Then—thank you. And bite me."

His scowl changed to a laugh. "As tempting as that sounds…"

The look she shot him stopped the words, but his smile remained in place.

The hotel room was large and beautifully decorated. A sitting area at one side included a comfortable-looking, chintz-covered sofa, a low coffee table decorated with an arrangement of fresh flowers and two side chairs holding pretty porcelain-based lamps. Set into a bow window was a small, round wood table flanked by two straight-back chairs with flowered cushions. A carved headboard accented the big bed, and the ruffled, fluffy-looking bed coverings invited a weary traveler to rest.

The color scheme was a restful dark green with touches of burgundy and cream to keep the overall effect from being too dark. Even the artwork was unusually pleasing for a hotel room, good-quality prints of impressionist masterpieces.

But Jessica was too irritated to appreciate either the room or the breathtaking view from the big window.

Waiting only until the bellhop had deposited the bags, accepted her tip and slipped out the door, she whirled on Sam, who stood in the center of the room looking braced for a battle. "The only reason we didn't have this quarrel downstairs is because I didn't want to cause a scene and risk being thrown out of the hotel, but now I can say exactly what I want. If you think I'm going to share a hotel room with you, you're crazy."

"You heard the guy downstairs. He said it in both French and English. There are no more rooms here, and chances are slim that I'd find a room anywhere else in Lausanne this weekend with the jazz festival going on."

"That's your problem, not mine."

"Jessica, be reasonable. This is a big room. I'll sleep on the couch. We're only going to be here a night or two, until after your visit with your mother."

The reminder of her mother had her shaking her head again, this time more firmly. As far as she was concerned, having Sam move to another hotel was the ideal solution. She would be more likely to slip away from him that way, if necessary. "I'm not sharing a room with you."

He shrugged. "Then I guess I'll sleep in the car. Won't be the first time."

She pictured the tiny vehicle they had rented in Geneva. There was barely room for a man of Sam's size to sit up fully, much less stretch out to sleep. "You can't sleep in the car."

"Doesn't look as though I have a choice, does it?"

"You could find another hotel. With your knowledge of this area and your fluency in the language, I'm sure you'd have no problem."

"The problem would be that even if I could find another place to stay, I would be leaving you alone here. No bodyguard worth his salt would sleep in a separate hotel from his client."

"I told you, I don't want or need a bodyguard."

"And I told *you* that you have one, whether you like it or not. So—I'll sleep in the car."

"Darn it, Sam, you aren't going to make me feel guilty. I had a reservation here."

"True. There's no reason for you to feel guilty."

She sighed and resisted a childish impulse to stamp her foot. "You'll sleep on the couch. And if you snore, I'll throw a shoe at your head."

"I don't snore."

She decided she didn't want to talk anymore about their sleeping arrangements. They would deal with that when it became necessary.

She glanced at her watch. "It's past lunchtime. I'm hungry. And then I want to find my mother."

"We can do that. How about fresh fish from Lac Léman? It's a specialty around here, and I highly recommend it."

That quickly, he'd gone from implacable bodyguard mode to charming tour guide again. She pushed a hand through her hair and sighed lightly, wondering how her carefully laid plans had taken such strange twists in the past three days. "Fine. We'll eat fish."

He motioned toward the door. "Then let's go."

She had taken only one step toward the door when the telephone on the nightstand beside the bed suddenly rang.

Chapter Nine

Jessica looked quickly at Sam, who stood closer to the phone than she did.

His eyebrows rose. "You want me to answer?"

She almost said yes. She tried to convince herself it was because he was more fluent in the local languages, but she knew it was pure cowardice that made her so reluctant to reach for the phone.

Because she was determined to overcome the fears that had plagued her for so much of her life, she squared her shoulders and reached for the receiver. "I'll get it."

Sam nodded and moved back across the room, giving her some space but staying close by.

"Hello?"

Cade exploded into speech the moment he heard her

voice. "What the hell are you doing in Lausanne? And why didn't you tell anyone where you were going?"

"How did you find me?" she asked her eldest brother rather than answering his questions. "Did Dad tell you?"

Cade and Walter had barely spoken since Cade had defied their father to leave the prestigious law firm Walter had encouraged him to join, but Jessica wouldn't put it past her father to contact Cade if he thought there was an advantage to him in doing so.

"Yeah, he called," Cade admitted reluctantly. "He said you'd run off to Switzerland on some quest to see our mother. He wanted me to talk to you and convince you to come home, but it took this long just to track you down."

"Yes, well, I had a few unexpected delays on the trip. I've only just arrived in Lausanne."

"I can't believe you did this. Do you know how vulnerable you are alone over there? Hell, you've hardly ever left San Francisco. Anything could have happened to you already, and we wouldn't even have known had Dad not given me a warning of what you were up to."

"And just how did *he* know?" she challenged, wondering exactly what Cade had been told.

Cade hesitated. "He's had someone watching you," he admitted at last, sounding braced for a temper tantrum. "I don't blame you for hating that, but he said he was doing it for your own good. You know I don't trust his motives any more than you do, but with everything in the family so chaotic now, we all have to take extra precautions."

"Oh? Does that mean he's hired a bodyguard for you? Or for Rowan? Emily doesn't count, I guess, since she's got more bodyguards than shoes now that she's royalty."

Cade cleared his throat. "Rowan and I can take care of ourselves."

"And I can't, is that it?"

"The fact that you're there at all proves you need *someone* looking after you, and since we don't know if Dad's bodyguard is still on the job or not, I'm worried about you. You shouldn't be there alone."

Jessica glanced at Sam, but something made her keep quiet about his presence in the room with her. He had his back turned to her now, and he was looking out the window at the breathtaking scenery outside, but she had no doubt he heard every word she was saying.

Choosing her words carefully, she said, "You don't need to worry about me, Cade. I'm fine. I simply wanted a chance to see our mother. Surely you can understand that, even if you don't share the desire."

"I didn't say I don't understand—I just think your timing's bad, that's all. With Dad in so much trouble now, and every move we make being watched and an-alyzed, how's it going to look for you to bolt during the trial to visit our crazy mother? You've heard the recent rumors that Dad had her put away because she knew too much about his allegedly illegal activities."

"Allegedly illegal," she repeated with a bitter taste in her mouth. "Stop being such a lawyer, Cade. You and I both know there's a very good chance that his activities were more than *allegedly* illegal. And it may be that Mother knows more about them than he wants us to hear."

"I'm afraid you're going to be disappointed when you

see her. She hasn't seen you since you were a baby, and she was too lost in her depression and alcoholism and whatever other problems she suffered to take care of you then. You have no way of knowing if anything she'll tell you is true or a product of her troubled imagination."

"And maybe I'll find out that she isn't as crazy as we've been told she is."

There was sympathy in Cade's voice when he replied, "Don't set yourself up for heartbreak, Jess. Have you thought about how you'll handle it if the meeting is a total disaster? Are you going to be able to…well, you know. Get over it?"

"You mean am I going to have a total breakdown and end up locked in a padded room, myself? Gee, I don't know. I suppose it's a definite possibility."

"Damn it, that isn't what I meant, and you know it."

"Do I?" There was as much sadness as bitterness in her voice now, and she was well aware of it. She was so tired of fighting the doubts. Her family's. And her own.

"Come home, Jessie. Or if you have to do this, let me join you there. I'll go with you to see her."

"No. I don't want to wait now that I'm here. Besides, you have too much going on there. I can handle this. No matter what happens. And don't worry about my safety, either. I'm—" she glanced again at Sam, then finished "—I'm taking precautions."

"What kind of—"

"Goodbye, Cade. I'll call you when I have something to tell you." She could hear him still talking rapidly as she replaced the receiver in its cradle.

She kept her back to Sam after she hung up, hoping

she would have her expression under control by the time she turned to face him. She didn't want him to see how badly her conversation with Cade had shaken her.

She should have known he didn't have to see her face. He had proven himself to be uncannily perceptive when it came to her.

His hands fell on her shoulders before she even realized he had moved to stand behind her. The guy really should make some sort of noise when he walked, she thought grumpily.

"Are you okay?"

"I'm fine. I just don't like to quarrel with my brother."

"Have you thought of reminding him that you're twenty-six years old and you don't need his permission to do anything you want to do?"

"Sometimes that message is a little hard to get through to him. To any of them. Maybe if I'd started acting like an adult a little sooner…"

"So you had a couple of setbacks. Considering everything, you seem to be doing pretty well to me."

"Just your average head case," she quipped with a short laugh that didn't quite come off.

His hands tightened abruptly on her shoulders, not quite to the point of pain. "Damn it, Jessica, stop saying things like that. It isn't funny."

She stared straight ahead at the blank wall in front of her. "There are some people who would tell you it wasn't a joke. That it's simply the truth."

"They would be wrong."

"Some of them know me pretty well."

"Not if they think you're a 'head case,' they don't."

She crossed her arms tightly in front of her. "Maybe they've seen things you haven't. Sometimes I do things—well, you saw me walk in front of that car…"

"Jessica." He spoke right into her ear now, his head almost resting against hers, standing so close behind her she could feel the warmth of him. "Being occasionally absentminded or careless—especially in times of stress—is not abnormal. You should have seen me when my marriage ended. I had trouble remembering to eat or shave—all I could focus on was my anger."

She moistened her dry lips with the tip of her tongue. She had never talked about her fears with anyone, not even Emily or Caroline. Why was she suddenly tempted to spill all to a man who was barely more than a stranger to her?

"The difference is that your mother didn't spend your whole life in a mental institution," she said so quietly it was almost a whisper. "And you didn't grow up hearing yourself compared to her every day."

"My father was an alcoholic. He stayed sober on the job, but headed for the nearest bar as soon as his shift was over. He was addicted to booze and women, and from the day I entered the police academy, my mother predicted I would end up following in all his footsteps. I haven't, but don't think I haven't worried about the tendencies I might have inherited from him."

Just like the first time he'd shared a glimpse of his past with her, what he told her made her feel a bit closer to him. Made her want to believe that she had found someone who understood—at least a little—what it was like to live in fear of one's own genes.

"At least you have a choice not to start drinking. What if—"

"What if what?" he asked gently.

She drew a deep breath, then blurted it out. "What if I look into my mother's eyes today and realize that she really does have serious mental problems? How can I know for sure that I won't end up just like her? That I'm not already headed in that direction?"

He turned her to face him. His hands still on her shoulders, he held his face close to hers. "It doesn't matter if you find out your mother is a raving lunatic. *You are not crazy,* Jessica."

"But how do you know?"

"I know because I've looked into *your* eyes."

His right hand was against her cheek now. His palm was so warm against her skin, his touch so comforting. She felt her breath catch as she found herself suddenly lost in Sam's heated jade gaze.

It took an effort for her to form coherent words. "I— haven't told you everything."

He shrugged. "That doesn't surprise me. We've only spent a couple of days together. There are a lot of things we don't know about each other. But I do know that you're as sane as I am—for whatever that's worth."

She swallowed hard, warning herself to be cautious. Yes, there was a certain appeal in finding someone who seemed to understand her in a way few other people had. And, yes, it was easy to feel as though their mutual experiences with difficult and absent parents created a bond of sorts between them. And, okay, the guy had absolutely gorgeous eyes. But still…

His smile had faded now, to be replaced by an expression that was rather stern. His left hand still rested on her shoulder, and she felt his fingers tighten in a reflexive movement as he used his other hand to trace the line of her jaw. His gaze was focused on her mouth now, and she felt her lips tremble when she imagined what it would be like to kiss him.

"Sam?" she whispered.

He ran his thumb very lightly across her lower lip. "Mmm?"

"Maybe I am crazy, after all."

He frowned, and started to speak.

She rose on tiptoe and covered his mouth with her own, effectively muffling whatever he had intended to say.

And to think that Jessica had called herself "predictable." Had Sam not been so very preoccupied with kissing her, he might have laughed.

Her mouth was as delicious as he had imagined when he'd studied it so intently during the past few days. Her body felt as good in his arms as he remembered from dancing too briefly with her the night before.

He hadn't expected her to kiss him, but since he'd been wanting to kiss her almost from the first time he had seen her, he couldn't say he was sorry she had. He suspected that it was a bad idea, all in all—but he didn't have the willpower to push her away.

Though powerful, the kiss didn't last long. Just as she had been the one to instigate it, Jessica was the one who brought it to an end.

She lowered herself from her tiptoes and dropped the

hands she had splayed on his chest, her lips separating slowly from his. He didn't try to detain her, as much as he would have liked to keep her there longer.

Remembering what she'd said just before she kissed him, he gave her a smile that felt decidedly crooked. "If that was crazy, I'm all for it."

He hadn't been sure how she would react to the attempt at a joke. He was relieved when she laughed lightly. Pushing a hand through her hair, she half turned away. "It *was* crazy. But it was pleasant."

"Pleasant?" He frowned, not sure he liked that description.

"Oh, stuff your ego in your pocket and take me to lunch, Fields."

"Okay—but maybe later we can try for better than pleasant?"

"Don't hold your breath. That was a onetime thing— a thank-you for being so nice."

Following her out of the room, Sam resolved to be as "nice" as possible for the remainder of the day.

They dined in a lovely café in Ouchy, at the bottom of Lausanne's sharply rising terrain. Once a fishing village, Ouchy was now a prime spot for strolling along the waterfront and admiring the mountains rising to the north.

Jessica lingered over her meal, her gaze turning often to the windows. As lovely as it was in the winter, she would love to visit in the summertime. She could very easily fall in love with Switzerland.

Some impulse made her glance at Sam then, and she caught him smiling at her. There was a place deep inside her that always started to tingle whenever she saw that particular smile.

She could very easily fancy herself in love with him, too, if she wasn't extremely careful. She was vulnerable, he seemed sympathetic; she had felt isolated for too long, and he claimed to understand her. And there was no denying the physical attraction between them.

No matter what he really thought of her, she couldn't mistake the appreciation in the way he looked at her. And in the way he had held her and kissed her.

"I'd almost forgotten how much I like it here," he said, obviously making conversation to take her mind off her worries. "The Geneva-Lausanne area has always been my favorite. I've heard the snow is just getting perfect for the skiing season, even though it has been a bit warmer than usual here at lake level."

The weather. Okay, there was a safe topic. "I've noticed it's been quite mild since we arrived. I expected to have to bundle up more than I have."

"The temperatures depend on the elevation, of course. If you travel only ten kilometers northeast, you'll find yourself nearly six hundred meters higher than you are here. It's much cooler there, of course."

"I'm sure it's lovely there."

"Yes, it is. Would you like to chat about how good our food is now, or do you want to tell me why you're trying to stretch this meal out as long as you can?"

She made a face. "I guess it's pretty obvious that I've been stalling."

"Yeah. You've pushed that same last bite of fish around your plate for the past ten minutes."

She set her fork down. "You're right. We should go."

"It will be all right, Jessica. Whatever you find out about your mother, you can deal with it."

"I know. I'm just…nervous."

"Understandably so." He tossed his napkin on the table beside his plate. "The longer we sit here, the more nervous you're going to get."

She nodded, drew a deep breath and rose to her feet. Sam was right. She had come all this way, and now it was time to find out some long-overdue truths.

The asylum wasn't as easy to find as the hotel had been. Even though Jessica had the address, in a village about ten kilometers west of Lausanne, the asylum was extremely secluded, located well off the main tourist path.

Having asked around a little, Sam had discovered that this was a place where the wealthy stashed their embarrassments. The schizophrenic son, the severely neurotic daughter, the uncle who thought he was Bonaparte and the aunt who talked to her cats—and thought they talked back. Or, in Jessica's case, the depressed, alcoholic, bipolar mother.

The place looked much like one of the exclusive resorts in nearby Montreaux. The main building was large and impressive, accessed by a sweeping circular drive. The grounds behind the building were fenced, but landscaped to downplay the heavy security. In the summer, Sam imagined that the lawns would be very green and probably covered in flowers. Now they were prettily dusted with snow.

"Nice place."

Jessica's face wore little expression as she looked around. "Yes, well, I've learned from experience that even the most beautiful locations can still be prisons."

She was talking about her own home, of course. Another immaculately landscaped estate in which there had been little joy for her.

Sam parked in a space marked for visitors, then rounded the car to open Jessica's door for her. It was a sign of her trepidation that she waited for him to do so; usually, she opened her own door and was out of the car almost before he cut the engine.

Feeling how cold her fingers were when he helped her out of the car, he wrapped his warmer hand around hers. He didn't let go as he escorted her up the sweeping steps to the front entrance, nor did she try to pull away. She seemed to appreciate the gesture of support.

He tried not to read too much into her holding on to him. Chances were she'd have clung to anyone who offered encouragement at that moment.

A marble-floored entryway led to a massive front desk. No one would enter the building without stopping there first, Sam noted, spotting signs of security everywhere.

A very professional-looking woman with black eyes and severely cut black hair sat behind the desk typing something into a computer. She wore a telephone headset, and she swung the transmitter away from her mouth when she greeted them. "Bonjour."

Jessica glanced at Sam. Taking her sudden attack of muteness as a sign that she would like his help, he flashed the charming smile he reserved for ferocious receptionists and secretaries. "Bonjour. Parlez-vous anglais?"

She waggled a hand. "Un petit peu."

Because he figured Jessica would be more comfortable if the conversation were conducted in English, he switched, speaking clearly. "My name is Sam Fields. This is my friend, Jessica Parks. She's here to visit her mother."

One perfectly arched black eyebrow lifting, the woman studied Jessica. "Your mother?" she repeated in heavily inflected English.

Jessica nodded, visibly relieved to be able to speak. "Anna Parks. She's a patient here."

"You are expected?"

"No. I'm afraid this is a spur-of-the-moment visit."

The woman frowned. "Je ne comprends pas."

"I'm not expected."

"Then you are not on ze list."

"No. But I've come all the way from America. Surely something can be arranged. Maybe I could speak to her doctor and get permission to see her?"

"Anna Parks?"

Jessica let go of Sam's hand to rest both of hers on the massive desk. "Yes."

The woman typed something into the computer, then shook her head. "No visitors."

"What do you mean, no visitors?"

Both eyebrows lifting in response to Jessica's suddenly raised voice, the woman turned away from the computer screen. "No visitors."

Suspecting he detected Walter's involvement here, Sam stepped up again. "Pardon—Quel est votre nom?"

Looking at him suspiciously, she gave her name. "Chantal DuBois."

"Mademoiselle DuBois?"

"Oui."

Increasing the wattage of his smile, he leaned against the desk and looked directly into her eyes. Speaking in French, he explained Jessica's situation, laying it on a bit thickly as he described her lifelong desire to see her mother, her long journey, the exhausting delays along the way. "Is there nothing you can do to help us?"

Chantal's pale face took on the faintest pink tinge. "Perhaps I could make a call. I don't know why this no visitors restriction has been added this weekend. There are only two people on her list of regular visitors, outside her doctors, of course."

"Can you tell me who those approved visitors are?"

"I'm not really supposed to—"

Sam leaned a little closer to her. "I assure you I will keep your assistance in confidence, Chantal. This is very important to my friend. And to me."

Chantal cleared her throat and glanced back at the computer monitor. "Her friend, Madame Bressoux. And her son, Mr. Ross."

Sam frowned. "You mean, her friend's son?"

"No. Madame Parks's son." Chantal stopped suddenly, as if concerned that she had said too much. "I assumed you—I'll try to call Dr. Rouiller."

Jessica tugged at Sam's jacket sleeve when Chantal turned away. "Well? What did she say?"

"I think she might be a bit confused." He summed up his conversation with the receptionist.

Jessica was shaking her head before he finished

speaking. "She *must* be confused. Neither of my brothers have ever visited my mother here."

"She called him Mr. Ross," Sam reminded her.

"That's Derek's last name. He told me he's never visited her here." She swallowed visibly and shook her head again. "It must be a mistake."

"I'm sure you're right. Maybe she meant your mother is occasionally visited by a friend and the friend's son—whose first name could be Ross. I'll admit it's a coincidence, but certainly possible."

"I suppose... Still, I don't know who they could be."

"Your mother has lived here for twenty-five years. It's entirely probable that she has made a friend or two while she was here."

"Yes. I'm sure you're right." She hesitated a moment. "This new restriction against visitors. My father arranged that, didn't he?"

"Very likely. I suppose it's all he could do, since he couldn't physically stop you from coming here."

She tilted her chin, her eyes flashing. "He won't stop me from seeing her. If I have to fight my way in, I *will* see her."

"Anyone ever tell you you're incredibly sexy when you're so fierce?"

"Pig."

He chuckled, then turned back to the desk when Chantal said, "I'm sorry, but Dr. Rouiller is unavailable today. I cannot give permission to enter without his approval."

"I want to see my mother," Jessica insisted, slapping both hands on the reception desk. "I've come all this way and I'm not going home without seeing her."

"If we could speak to someone in charge?" Sam suggested. "Someone with authority to approve a visit?"

"That would be difficult today. There is no one available. Regular weekly visitation is tomorrow afternoon. If you could come back then?"

"Tomorrow?" Jessica repeated. She looked at him then. "But, Sam, we're so close."

"I know. You want to fight your way in. I understand. But maybe it's best if we wait until tomorrow, as she suggested. We have a better chance of getting in if we play along at first."

"I'm not going home without seeing my mother," Jessica said stubbornly.

"I know," he assured her. "One way or another, we'll get you in. Tomorrow."

Though he could see how much it cost her, she nodded reluctantly. "I seem to have no other choice."

Chapter Ten

Jessica's steps were dragging a bit when they returned to the car. Sam knew she had to be bitterly disappointed.

"You'll see her tomorrow," he promised again as she fastened her seat belt.

"He's doing everything he can to stop me."

"Yes. But there's only so much he can do to interfere from a California jail cell. And other than being here when he's not, you do have one other advantage."

"What's that?"

"Me."

She clasped her hands in her lap and remained silent. After a moment, Sam cleared his throat. "Jessica?"

Without looking at him, she responded, "What?"

"You do believe that I'm going to help you, don't you?"

There was another pause before she said, "So you keep telling me."

"You don't sound overly confident."

Slanting him a sideways glance, she murmured, "It has occurred to me that I don't really know what you were saying to that woman when you were speaking French."

It took an effort for him to hold on to his patience and disguise his irritation when he answered steadily, "I told you word for word what we said."

Again, she said nothing.

Setting his back teeth together, Sam leaned a bit closer to her. "If I were going to try to stop you from seeing your mother, you never would have gotten this far."

"I'd have gotten here. Just like I'm going to see her tomorrow. By whatever means necessary."

"I believe you. And I'm on your side, Jessica. I want you to start believing that."

Still looking disgruntled, she pushed her hair out of her face and looked out the window at the few other cars parked around them. "This trip is costing a fortune. It's just one delay after another."

"Since you've risked everything to get here, you might as well take advantage of your visit," he said, driving away from the asylum and aware that Jessica was looking wistfully back as they pulled away. "How would you like to see a real twelfth-century castle? The Château de Chillon sits in the middle of Lake Geneva. It's been restored, and it's filled with tapestries and other artifacts."

She looked at him with a faint spark of interest. "I've never been in a real castle before."

"Then we should definitely go. It's not as if we have anything else to do to kill time until tomorrow."

"I think I'd like that."

Jessica Parks hadn't played nearly enough in recent years—if ever, he decided. And since he had been accused on more than one occasion of playing a bit too much, he was just the man to remind her of how to have a little fun.

It was very late by the time Jessica walked back into her hotel room. All too aware of Sam following closely behind her, she shrugged out of her black down coat and laid it over the back of a chair.

The red sweater and black slacks she had worn for the planned visit with her mother still looked fresh, despite the busy day. Fortunately, her black boots were comfortable, since she and Sam had done a great deal of walking that afternoon.

When she had been forced to leave the asylum in such bitter disappointment, she never would have expected that she would end up enjoying the rest of the day so much. She hadn't come to Switzerland on vacation, but Sam had given her the full tourist treatment that afternoon and evening. Castles and galleries, shops and châteaus—he had shown her all of them, and she'd had a wonderful time.

She hadn't brought a camera with her on this trip, but she had stored dozens of photographs in her head. She was well aware that Sam would always be predominant in most of those mental pictures.

He had been the perfect companion. Knowledgeable

of the area and the languages, going out of his way to make sure she had a nice time. They had eaten local delicacies and listened to excellent jazz. They'd danced again. And most surprisingly to Jessica, they had laughed. *She* had laughed, more than she had in a long time.

Who would have believed it?

Sam locked the door behind him. The sound of the latch snapping home made her heart leap into her throat. She swallowed, trying not to gulp.

"Man, I'm beat." His voice was cheerfully impersonal as he headed toward the sofa. "I haven't done the tourist thing in years. This sofa looks inviting right now."

She smoothed her hands down her sides. "Maybe you should take the bed. You're really too tall for the sofa."

"I'll be fine. This is your room. You get the bed."

"But—"

"You'll take the bed."

It was the first time all day he had used that particular tone. The one that let her know she would be wasting her breath to argue. "And," he added, "you can take the first bathroom shift. Take your time, I'm going to sit and stretch my legs out for a bit."

Deciding to concede with dignity, she gathered her things and locked herself in the bathroom.

As Sam had suggested, she took her time changing into her most conservative yellow flannel pajamas, washing her face and brushing her teeth. It felt so strange to know Sam waited in the other room. That she would be crawling into bed with him only a few feet away.

Part of the purpose of this trip had been to prove herself a capable, independent woman. She had done a lot of things she'd never done before. Traveled by herself—at least for the first leg of the journey. Slept in an airport. Dined and danced in Zurich and Lausanne. Toured an ancient castle and sensed the ghosts in the shadows.

Spending the night in a hotel room with a man—even in separate beds—was another first for her, though there was no need for Sam to know that.

Perhaps she had been a bit too focused on her family problems during the past few years. A little too obsessed with her plans. Somewhat too wary and suspicious of the motives of every man she met. She had dated occasionally. But there had been no serious relationships. Not even casual affairs. And now that lack of experience made her worry that she was too susceptible to Sam's sexy smiles and flattering attentions.

The fact that he performed his duties with charm and enthusiasm shouldn't blind her to the reality of the situation.

She didn't meet Sam's eyes as she moved out of the bathroom and straight toward the bed. "It's all yours."

He straightened from the sofa, where he had spread an extra blanket and propped a pillow at one end. "That was quick."

"Yes, well, I'm tired."

"Good night, then. Go ahead and turn out the lights, if you want. I can find my way in the dark."

She never slept with all the lights off. Ever since her kidnapping, when the nights had been much too long and too dark, she'd slept with at least a night-light burning somewhere nearby. Because she was making such an effort to prove herself an adult now, she rather defiantly turned off the lights in the hotel room, hoping that at least a glimmer of light would seep through the draperies.

But the heavy fabrics did their job. The room was plunged into total darkness, without even a crack of light showing beneath the closed bathroom door. Jessica felt her breath catch in her throat. She sank into the pillows and pulled the covers to her chin, reminding herself that Sam was only a few feet away. And then hating herself because that reminder made her feel better immediately.

She heard the bathroom door open, but Sam had already turned out the lights in there. Evidently he had eyes like a cat, because she heard him move to the sofa without stumbling, which was more than she could have accomplished.

She listened to the sounds of him settling onto the sofa, and she knew his feet must be hanging off the end. She considered offering him the bed again, but he'd made it clear that he had no intention of taking it. She closed her eyes and released a long, silent breath, willing herself to sleep.

It didn't work. She could almost feel the minutes ticking slowly past as she lay there, staring blindly up at the ceiling and wishing for daylight. Her mind raced with thoughts she couldn't put away. Thoughts of her mother. Of her uncertain future. Of the man lying on the sofa on the other side of the room.

She jumped when Sam spoke. "Would you be more comfortable if I turn on a light in the bathroom?"

Automatically going on the defensive, she replied, "I don't need a light."

"I could tell you were uncomfortable when I suggested you turn off the lights. It's no big deal, you know. Lots of people sleep with night-lights."

"I just don't sleep well in strange surroundings. Maybe I'm a little too keyed up about tomorrow."

"Is it because I'm here that you can't sleep? Because I can still move down to the car...."

"No," she said a bit too quickly. "There's no need for you to leave."

She hoped he didn't interpret her quick rejection of the suggestion to mean she didn't want to be alone tonight—even though that was exactly what she did mean. "I'm just a little worried about tomorrow, that's all. Concerned about how hard they'll fight to keep me from seeing my mother. And of course, I'm a bit nervous about when I do see her, and what she'll be like. And I can't help thinking about what will happen when I go back to San Francisco—what's going to happen with Dad and all. It's only natural that I'd have a little trouble sleeping tonight. I'm sorry if I'm keeping you awake."

"I'd find it hard to sleep, too, if I were about to meet my mother for the first time."

She rolled to her right side, trying to get comfortable.

"Jessica?"

"Mmm?"

"About what you said in the car this afternoon. Your implication that you still weren't sure you could trust me to help you see your mother?"

She winced. "Um—yeah, about that. I was mad, of course, that I'd been turned away. And disappointed that I hadn't been able to see her. I guess I lashed out at you."

"Does that mean you trust me, after all?"

She bit her lower lip, wondering how she was supposed to answer that.

"Jessica?"

She didn't have to see his face to know he was frowning. "If I didn't trust you, would I be sleeping in the same room with you?"

"That does take a certain leap of faith. And don't think I'm not pleased that you trust me that much, at least. But it isn't really what I asked you."

"You want to know if I still think you're trying to stop me from seeing my mother."

"Right."

Maybe the darkness made it easier for her to be honest with him. "I can't figure out why you would suddenly be on my side when you were working for my father until two days ago. I don't know what's in it for you."

"You think there has to be something in it for me?"

Oddly enough, he sounded more curious than offended. "Yes," she said simply. "There's always an angle. I just haven't figured out what yours is, yet."

"He's really done a number on you, hasn't he? And I thought *I* was cynical."

She didn't have to ask who he was referring to. "I prefer to think of myself as realistic."

"Has it occurred to you that I might simply want to help you?"

"Why? You don't even know me."

"Maybe I'm getting to know you a little better than you think."

After a long stretch of silence, he laughed a little.

"That scares you, doesn't it? You don't want anyone to get to know you too well, do you?"

She moistened her lips. "Maybe there are things about me you wouldn't want to know."

"Back to that again, are we?" He sighed, then said in a deliberately weary voice, "You are not crazy."

"'I'm just a little unwell,'" she murmured, once again quoting her self-declared "theme song."

"Then maybe we're both crazy," he said roughly. "Because no matter how many arguments I give myself why I should stay away from you—your distrust of me being primary among them—I'd still give anything I have to be in that bed with you. And if that doesn't give you a clue about my reasons for being on your side in this, then you haven't been paying very close attention."

What was she supposed to say in response to *that?* She gnawed on her lower lip, telling herself that the same arguments applied for her. It really was a bad idea for her to even consider inviting him into her bed—but the images now flooding her mind were enough to melt her spine, much less her willpower.

She hadn't forgotten how good it had felt just to kiss him. She couldn't even imagine what it must be like to make love with him.

"Go to sleep, Jessica," he said, and this time his weariness sounded genuine. "We'll deal with our problems tomorrow, after we've had some rest."

At least Sam had taken her mind off her family problems, Jessica thought as she nestled more deeply into the bed coverings. Now all she could think about was him.

* * *

Jessica was surprised to open her eyes and realize that she had managed a full seven hours of sleep. The clock on the bedside table told her it was 7:30 a.m. She lifted her head to see if Sam was still sleeping.

The sofa was empty. The blanket he had used was folded neatly at one end, with the pillow resting on top of it. The bathroom door stood open, and she could see that the room was empty. Where on earth had he gone?

There were signs in the bathroom that Sam had showered before going out. Though she tended to be a heavy sleeper, she was still surprised she hadn't roused when Sam had dressed and left the room. He really could move very quietly when he chose to do so.

She showered quickly, dried her hair, applied makeup and dressed in a peacock-blue sweater and a fresh pair of black slacks. To cut down on baggage, she had packed several pairs of black slacks and mix-and-match tops.

Sam was waiting when she came out of the bathroom. Because his cheeks were still a bit cold-reddened when he turned away from the table in the window to greet her, she figured he hadn't been back for long.

"Good morning," he said. "You look nice."

Suddenly remembering the things he had said to her in the darkness last night, she tucked a strand of hair behind her ear in a self-conscious gesture. "Thank you. What are you doing?"

He stepped to one side to give her a better look at the table behind him. A tall white taper in a crystal holder sat in the center, next to a single white rose in a crystal bud vase. Two snowy linen placemats were set with white china plates and cups, silverware and linen napkins. A cut glass plate held an assortment of delicious-looking pastries, surrounded by plump strawberries, and a white carafe stood next to the plate.

She smiled. "This looks wonderful."

He lifted one shoulder, looking rather pleased with himself. "I remembered a good bakery that I used to visit here. I wasn't sure it was still in business, but it looked exactly the way I remembered it."

He leaned over to light the candle with a pocket lighter. "As for the rest of the things, I found a helpful hotel employee. She brought this stuff up for me. She left while your hair dryer was still running, which is probably why you didn't hear us moving around in here."

Sam seemed to have a knack for charming people into assisting him, she mused. She hoped that talent would come in handy when they went back to see her mother later.

"I can't believe you put all this together so quickly. I really didn't take all that long to get dressed."

He studied the table. "Something's missing—oh, wait. I know what it is."

With a flourish, he opened the draperies. Jessica caught her breath in delight. "It's snowing!"

Smiling as if he'd arranged that, too, he held her chair for her. "It started while I was at the bakery."

"Oh, it's beautiful." Sinking into her seat, she gazed out the bow window. "It's like having breakfast inside a snow globe."

"That's a pretty image. Not as pretty as the one I'm seeing, of course."

She glanced away from the window to find him smiling at her from across the tiny table. The candlelight flickered between them, and she could smell the scent of the perfect white rose. The sheer romance of the moment made her catch her breath.

It should have seemed heavily orchestrated on his part; instead, it just seemed incredibly sweet. Which probably said a great deal about the way she had come to feel about him.

"You're very good at this, aren't you?"

He lifted an eyebrow. "At what?"

She waved a hand at the table settings, encompassing the candle, the rose, even the snowy window in the motion. "Charmingly romantic gestures."

His sudden frown looked genuine enough. "I wasn't trying to make a gesture. I just thought you might like a nice breakfast before we head out today."

Now she'd hurt his feelings. Oddly enough, she hadn't realized that she could.

"And I appreciate your thoughtfulness," she assured him quickly. "Everything is perfect. I just noticed that things like this seem to come naturally to you."

He was smiling again, though rather ruefully. "My ex-wife would tell you that I don't have a thoughtful bone in my body. Candlelight breakfasts aren't something I do all the time. It was just an impulse this morning after I bought the pastries. Something about the snow, I guess. Or just being here, in this elegant setting. Besides—"

"Besides, what?"

His expression was disarmingly sheepish when he replied, "I like to do nice things for you. I'm not sure that's something you've had enough of in your life."

Her cheeks warmed as she looked quickly down at her plate. The reference to his ex-wife had caused a little pang in her chest, but that feeling dissolved suddenly into a pleasant heat.

Sam could deny all he wanted that he was good at being romantic, but as far as she was concerned, he was a genius at it. How else could he have slipped so easily beneath the defenses she had erected against him?

"You make me a little nervous sometimes," she murmured, knowing her words were an understatement.

"Good. Because you scare the hell out of me."

She looked at him then, but he gave her a crooked smile and shook his head. "Let's just enjoy our breakfast, shall we? Pass me your cup."

She did so, then watched as he poured from the carafe. "I thought you'd brought coffee."

"Hot Swiss chocolate," he corrected her. "What else would you have with these fine French pastries?"

"I suppose I shouldn't even think about calories during this meal?"

"Absolutely not." He handed her the steaming cup of chocolate. "Sometimes it feels really good to be bad."

She eyed him over the rim of the cup, wondering if he was referring to anything other than breakfast. She couldn't tell from his blandly innocent expression.

Whatever his meaning, he was certainly right, she discovered quickly enough. It did feel wonderful to be bad. Sitting there in that window with the snow falling outside, a handsome, attentive man across the table, flaky pastries melting on her tongue and rich chocolate sliding down her throat, she was able to forget everything that had been bothering her for so long.

Just for that brief interlude, she was someone else. She wasn't being gawked at because her notorious father was in prison and her mother in an institution, or because her sister had married a king. Or because she was a bit odd herself.

She saw none of those things in Sam's eyes when he smiled at her across the table. Instead, there was an unmistakable masculine appreciation. An interest in what she had to say. Even respect for her opinions.

At that moment, she was just Jessica. And being valued for no other reason was much more seductive than the candlelight and flowers. More intoxicating than the smoothest of compliments.

She didn't want the novelty to end too quickly. "How long do we have until the maids come to clean?"

"I put the Do Not Disturb sign on the doorknob. We have as long as we want." Leaning a bit closer to her, he held out a hand. "Try this strawberry. I know they're technically out of season, but these are delicious."

She was tempted to take a bite while he held the berry, but since that seemed a bit dangerous, she reached up, instead, to pluck it from his fingers. "Mmm," she said a moment later. "That really is good."

His gaze focused on her mouth. He sounded quite distracted when he murmured, "Yeah. They're…good."

She swallowed hard in response to the look in his eyes. "Um—Sam…"

Still looking at her mouth, he sighed. "I'm trying to

behave. You make it difficult sometimes. You're so damn beautiful. I just thought you should know."

Her cheeks were probably bright red now, from the way they felt. Her hands weren't quite steady when she gripped them in her lap beneath the table. "When you say things like that…"

"I know," he cut in ruefully. "It makes it hard for you to start trusting me, doesn't it?"

"No," she said, wrinkling her nose in a self-deprecating expression. "It makes me want to kiss you again."

"Well, damn."

She had to smile at that, though it was a shaky effort. "I just thought you should know."

He cleared his throat. "You're trying to torture me, is that it?"

"You probably deserve it. But, as it happens, I'm just being honest."

He stood abruptly. "If you're finished with your breakfast, we'd probably better get out of here soon."

Jessica jumped to her feet—and promptly stumbled. Sam reached out to catch her, reminding her forcibly of the times she had done something foolish when he'd been following her around San Francisco. It was hard to believe it had been only a few days since she had considered him her enemy rather than her ally.

She wasn't even sure when she had started believing he was on her side. As late as last night, she had still been battling doubts about his motives. Had it taken nothing more than a few held glances over pastries and chocolate to win her over?

"You okay?" he asked, his hands still resting on her shoulders.

"I—" She looked up into his eyes and promptly forgot what she'd been about to say.

Sam muttered something she didn't understand. Before she could ask him to repeat it, his mouth was on hers.

Chapter Eleven

Sam pulled her closer as he deepened the kiss. He wanted her, she thought with a catch in her throat. Judging from the evidence, he wanted her badly. Could anything be more seductive for a woman who had spent most of her life wondering if she was truly wanted by anyone?

Her name rumbled in his throat as he tilted his head to kiss her from a new angle.

She had come on this trip at least partly to prove herself an adult. To stop living like a frightened child and make her own decisions. Her own mistakes, if necessary.

Perhaps Sam would eventually fall under the latter heading, but for now she wanted to know what it was to feel like a woman. She suspected that he was just the man to teach her.

Gathering her courage, she nestled closer to him, savoring the feel of his hard body against her softer curves. She touched her tongue to his, enjoying the taste of him.

His groan rumbled deep in his chest, vibrating against her sensitized breasts. She couldn't resist rubbing herself lightly against him, which made him groan again, more deeply this time.

"Jessica," he said, lifting his mouth from hers with obvious reluctance. "We really should stop this now."

"Stop protecting me, Sam. I don't need you to take care of me—not in this, or in anything else. And if you tell me again that it's your job to do so, I'll…I'll…"

He smiled faintly and touched a fingertip to her kiss-swollen lower lip. "What will you do?"

"Something that will make you sorry," she said, wishing she were able to come up with a more clever response.

The way he smiled gave her hope that she had gotten through to him. She didn't need a conscience or a keeper—and she sure didn't need another father.

"I think I mentioned before that I think you're just as cute as hell when you get all fierce and growly," he murmured.

"And I remembered that I called you a pig when you said that."

"I believe you did. So, does that mean you want me to keep my distance from you?"

"Is that what you want to do?"

His eyes darkened suddenly. His voice was gruff when he replied, "You know better than that."

"So, which one of us are you really protecting? Me—or yourself?"

"Damned if I know right now."

She reached up to rest her hands on his chest, leaning slightly toward him. "A wise man once told me that sometimes it feels really good to be bad." Lifting her mouth invitingly toward his, she added, "Let's see just how good we can feel."

Her new life had begun three days ago when she boarded a plane in Oakland. She didn't know where her quest for change would ultimately lead her, but she was eager to continue the journey.

She could almost hear him mentally listing the reasons they should walk away. But then he gave her a crooked smile and pulled her closer. "A wise man, hmm?"

"I might have been exaggerating a little…"

"Let's just leave it at that. I kind of like the sound of it." He spoke against her lips, his own curved into a smile. She looped her arms around his neck again and pulled his mouth more tightly against hers.

This time they left no space between them. She felt every inch of him pressed against her. The ripple of muscles in the arms that held her, the warmth of flesh beneath the fabric of his shirt. The ridge of his erection beneath his jeans. She felt her own body go limp and pliant in reaction.

He twisted to lower her to the bed, following her down. His weight pressed her deeply into the thick bed coverings, and she instinctively bent her knees upward to cradle him between them.

Now that she had convinced him she knew what she wanted—and that she wanted *him*—he seemed intent on proceeding without further delay. He slid her sweater over her head, tossing his shirt on the floor on top of it. Jessica barely had time to admire his bare chest—the line of his collarbone, the gold hairs that arrowed down to his navel, the deep hollow of his throat—before he moved to the waistband of her slacks.

Funny how she didn't feel self-conscious when he slid the fabric down her legs to leave her clad only in a black bra and panties. Not even when those scraps of lace joined the other clothing on the carpet next to the bed. She was too eager to experience more.

And Sam gave her more. The feel of his mouth on her throat, her breasts, her stomach. His hands at her hips, on her thigh, between her legs. His hairy legs rubbing against her smooth ones.

She wanted to believe she would have thought of protection before they went too far for it to matter. But it was Sam who took care of that detail, swiftly and matter-of-factly, digging the packets out of his bag.

She wanted to believe she was able to conceal the fact that this was her first experience with lovemaking, but she suspected he knew. Maybe it was the tentativeness of her movements, or the sheer wonder in her expression, but something gave her away.

Though he joined them carefully, there was no pain. Only pleasure. And when he started to move inside her, the pleasure built until she thought she would explode with it. Moments later, it felt very much as though she had.

Her startled cry was still echoing in the room when Sam followed her over the edge. She thought she had never heard anything more thrilling than the sound of her own name uttered in his broken gasp.

* * *

Maybe it had been a mistake. And he would probably pay for it later. But whatever the price, it would be worth it as far as Sam was concerned.

It wasn't that he had forgotten all the reasons he should have maintained a careful distance from Jessica. It was just that he had reached a point where none of those obstacles seemed to be insurmountable.

He knew why he'd made love with Jessica. After all, he had been fascinated by her from the first time he'd seen her. He had wanted her from the first time their eyes met—even if hers had been filled with anger. And when she had clutched his shirt so fiercely and told him she wanted him, too—well, hell. He was no saint.

So where did they go from here? Sitting behind the wheel of their little rental car, he slanted her a sideways glance. She had been distracted ever since they'd left the hotel room, which was understandable.

He cleared his throat. Waiting for her to bring up the subject was making him antsy. "It's a momentous day, hmm?" he asked, keeping his tone light.

"Yes. I've been giving it a lot of thought."

So, she had been thinking about their lovemaking, wondering where it would lead. "I guess you're wondering what's going to happen next."

"Of course. I just hope there's not a big scene."

He squirmed uncomfortably in his seat. "Well, there's no reason there should be, is there?"

"Only if they try to stop me from seeing her again. I'm not taking no for an answer this time."

"Oh. You were talking about your visit with your mother."

"Of course. What else?"

"Yeah. What else?" He kept his eyes focused on the windshield. The light snowfall earlier had stopped, for the most part, leaving only a light dusting on the roads, causing no driving problems. Still, he clenched the steering wheel a bit more tightly.

"I've made a decision. If they try to turn me away this time, I'll call my father. I'll tell him I'm not coming home until I see her, so he might as well give his permission."

She wore that fierce expression again, but Sam wasn't quite as amused by it this time. She was finding a bit too much satisfaction in openly defying her father for the first time in so long. Something about that observation bothered him.

Apparently satisfied that she'd made her point, she settled into her seat again with that same distracted expression from earlier. Knowing now that it was her mother who claimed her thoughts and not him, Sam made the rest of the drive with a scowl on his face.

The parking lot at the asylum was just a little more crowded than it had been the day before. Apparently, not many people took advantage of the regular weekly visitation hours, Sam mused. But then, he supposed he should have expected that from an institution known as a convenient place to stash embarrassing relatives.

The same woman was at the reception desk. She wore the same harried expression as yesterday as she faced a tall, rather arrogantly handsome young man with thick black hair, narrowed hazel eyes and an angry expression.

He spoke in French, his tone making it clear that he was accustomed to having his way. "I don't care what your computer says, I will see my mother, is that clear? You can either unlock that door for me, or you will get Dr. Rouiller on the telephone. Now."

"I'm sorry, Mr. Ross, but I have my instructions—"

The young man—Sam guessed him to be no older than twenty-five—leaned forward. "You have thirty seconds before I call my attorneys. I don't think the management will appreciate the legal problems they're going to encounter if I'm not let through those doors immediately."

Chantal DuBois quailed visibly. "I'll make a call."

"Good." Straightening away from the desk, the man pushed his hands into the pockets of his camel-hair coat and glowered at her, looking fully prepared to remain there as long as necessary.

"What's going on?" Jessica asked Sam in a low voice.

"This man is being denied permission to see his mother. Sound familiar?"

The man looked at them now, obviously having overheard and understood. "Have you encountered problems with visitation, as well?" he asked in perfect, if very slightly accented, English.

"My friend was turned away when she tried to visit her mother yesterday. We're here to try again."

The other man glanced automatically at Jessica. And then he did a visible double take, his jaw seeming to drop slightly. His voice was a bit strangled when he asked her, "Who is your mother?"

"Her name is Anna Parks. Do you know her?"

"Mon Dieu." It was little more than a whisper.

"We're told she looks exactly like her mother," Sam said, closely watching the other man's face.

"The resemblance is…uncanny."

Biting her lip, Jessica glanced at Sam, who wondered if he had already taken a few mental steps ahead of her to reach an unnerving suspicion.

The other man spoke again, his gaze still focused intently on Jessica's face. "May I ask your name?"

"I'm Jessica Parks. Oh, and this is my friend Sam Fields."

The offhanded way in which she had used the word *friend* made it sound to Sam roughly equivalent to "some guy I barely know and have no particular ties to." Or was he maybe being a bit too touchy?

"My name is Benton Ross." The young man studied Jessica's expression as he spoke, as if trying to determine if she had ever heard the name before.

Jessica frowned. "Your name was mentioned yesterday, in connection with my mother."

"Monsieur Ross?"

All three of them turned toward the reception desk in response to the receptionist's voice, but it was Benton who spoke. "Yes?"

Looking only at him, Chantal continued. "I spoke to Dr. Rouiller. He instructed me to allow you to go in."

Nodding in satisfaction, Benton turned to Jessica. "I will escort you to your mother."

Chantal shook her head rapidly. "I received permission only for you, Monsieur Ross. No other visitors have been approved."

Sam translated quietly for Jessica while Benton turned back to the desk. For a man so young, he had a definite air of authority about him. Not to mention a hint of threat when he spoke with icy control, "These people will accompany me. Do not try to interfere with me again."

Sam figured there was no need to translate that time. Benton's meaning was clear enough.

Chantal didn't actually throw up her hands, but her desire to do so was written in her exasperated expression. It was obvious that she had no interest in another battle—which she must surely have known would follow if she tried to bar Jessica from seeing her mother. "Fine," she said. "Take them with you."

Sam thought he heard her add beneath her breath, "It isn't worth it."

Jessica felt more as if she were inside a luxury resort than an asylum. Though the reception area had been formal, the inside was light and airy. Lots of greenery and fresh flowers, water trickling from built-in fountains, windows overlooking the fenced, but beautifully maintained grounds. It wasn't exactly the way she had envisioned her mother living for the past twenty-five years, but she was glad to see that this prison was a beautiful one, at least.

She cast a surreptitious glance at the man escorting them through the winding hallways, being greeted with familiarity by the few people they passed along the way. Benton Ross. An exceptionally handsome man with an air of wealth and subtle power that was familiar to her. But it was Benton's black hair and strong features that reminded her most vividly of someone.

He could very easily pose as a younger version of Derek Ross. Her mother's long-ago lover, she thought with a sudden pang of premonition.

They paused outside a door embellished with a wreath of grapevine and dried flowers. Benton reached out to knock on the door, but Jessica caught his arm to stop him. "Before we go in, would you please tell me who you are?"

Benton hesitated, then gave a slight shake of his head. "I think that would best be left to Madame," he murmured, and tapped lightly on the door.

"Entre."

Hearing the voice—her mother's voice—made Jessica's throat tighten. Without thinking, she reached out to Sam. He caught her hand in his, giving it a reassuring squeeze. Jessica noticed Benton watching them closely, and she nodded to indicate that she was ready.

They entered a spacious suite done in yellows and greens and light woods, so that it was almost like stepping from winter into summer. The sitting room was small, but inviting, with a big window overlooking a courtyard filled with birds flocking around hanging feeders. A closed door on one side of the room probably led into the bedroom. There didn't seem to be a kitchen, so Jessica assumed meals were served in a common dining room.

There were framed photographs on a low wooden sideboard. Jessica recognized several as pictures she had sent of herself and her siblings and her niece Stacy, Anna's grandchild. The others were all photographs of Benton Ross, from childhood to present.

Only after she had taken that brief moment to study the room—building her courage in the process—did she turn to the woman standing beside a wooden rocking chair that she had probably been sitting in prior to their arrival.

Anna Parks had been known for her beauty. Neither time nor adversity had taken that away from her. Her upswept blond hair was now streaked with gray, and there were a few lines on her face, but at fifty, she was still striking. Anna had been compared to Marilyn Monroe in her youth, whereas Jessica's curves were more delicate. Though age had added a few pounds, Anna was still a woman men would look twice at on the street.

Anna's blue eyes filled with tears as she gazed back at her daughter. "Jessica," she breathed. "You're here."

Jessica swallowed and managed a shy-feeling smile. "Hello, Mother."

"Oh, my baby." Anna was sobbing now, tears cascading down her cheeks. "You were only an infant when I saw you last. And now look at you. So beautiful."

Benton pulled a snowy handkerchief from his pocket and offered it to her. She accepted it with a teary smile and a murmured, "Thank you, darling."

Delicately wiping her eyes, Anna took a step toward Jessica, who hadn't moved. "You've met Benton?"

Jessica nodded slowly. "He's your son, isn't he?

Yours and Derek Ross's. Why didn't you tell me in your letters?"

"I thought it would be better to tell you in person."

"Does Derek know?"

"Yes. I wrote to him recently to inform him."

"Why didn't he tell me?"

"I asked him not to. I believe he has told his daughter, but I wanted to be the one to tell mine."

"Oh, my God." Jessica raised icy hands to her cheeks. "You had Derek Ross's child. I have another brother."

It seemed that half brothers were popping up out of the woodwork these days. She shook her head slowly at this further evidence of the dysfunctional and destructive nature of her parents' marriage. "You knew?" she asked Benton.

"I've seen your photographs. When I saw you downstairs, I knew who you must be."

"Please, let's all sit down," Anna said, looking flustered. "I'll try to explain."

She glanced at Sam, who had remained quietly in the background. "I don't believe we've been introduced…"

"My name is Sam Fields, Mrs. Parks."

"Please, call me Anna. You must be Jessica's boyfriend?"

"He's not my boyfriend," Jessica answered quickly. "He works for Dad."

Anna's eyes narrowed, her hardening expression giving the first evidence of her hatred for her husband. Jessica had known about that hostility from their letters, but now she got a glimpse of the full extent of the emotion.

Sam looked no more pleased by her words. He gave

her a look that contained both anger and a hint of hurt. "I *did* work for Walter Parks," he said evenly. "On a contract basis. I'm a private investigator he hired as a bodyguard for Jessica. Once she told me what she was trying to do, I decided to help her. I thought she had a right to see her mother, and that Walter had no right to try to interfere."

Anna didn't look particularly reassured. "You are no longer working for my husband?"

He met her eyes steadily. "No, I'm not."

Benton's face had taken on that threatening expression he had used with the receptionist earlier. "If I discover that you are working with him to hurt my mother, I will make you very sorry."

Jessica watched as Sam sighed and rubbed the back of his neck. "You suppose we could cut the melodrama?" he asked a bit wearily. "I'm not the bad guy here."

"He's right," Jessica said, regretting that she had overreacted to hearing her mother refer to Sam as her boyfriend. Once again, her unruly tongue had gotten her into trouble, and she'd taken Sam with her this time. "Sam was simply doing his job, taking care of me. And he has been very helpful in getting me this far."

"Please sit," Anna said again. "We must talk."

Once everyone was seated, Anna drew a deep breath, as if wondering where to start. She must have decided to start at the beginning.

"I was very young and vain when I met Walter," she said. "My life revolved around parties and discos, beauty pageants and the few acting roles that came my way. Walter romanced me with promises of wealth and popularity, and my father wanted the business alliance our marriage would form, so I allowed myself to be persuaded to marry him. My life changed almost as soon as the honeymoon began."

She went on to describe how Walter had begun to isolate her from her friends and even from her family. How he had assured her that he was only trying to protect her, but had basically confined her to their luxurious mansion, where she had spent too many hours alone.

"Sounds familiar," Jessica murmured, picturing her mother's life all too easily.

"It wasn't so bad once the twins and then Rowan came," Anna went on. "I adored my children. But Walter began to spend more time away, and I suspected there were other women. I was starved for adult companionship. I suffered from bouts of terrible depression that I tried to alleviate with alcohol and pills. That only made things worse, of course. Walter and I got into terrible fights. Twice I accidentally overdosed, and had to be rushed to the hospital. Walter began hinting to people that I was unstable and suicidal, which effectively kept my former friends away from me."

"Didn't you ever try to leave him?" Jessica asked.

Anna's shrug conveyed both regret and self-recrimination. "I was afraid of him," she said simply. "He was too powerful, and he would stop at nothing to have his way. He threatened to take my children away from me, so that I would never see them again. And he threatened to have me locked away. He would eventually go through with those threats, of course."

"Mrs. Parks, what happened the night Jeremy Carlton died?" Sam asked bluntly. "There's a rumor going around that you were sent away because you knew too much about Carlton's disappearance. Is that true?"

There was still distrust in Anna's gaze when she looked at Sam. Blaming herself for putting it there, Jessica spoke up. "I'd like to hear that, as well. Dad is in jail and Derek Ross is planning to testify that he saw Dad kill Carlton and throw his body off the side of a yacht. Dad's bookkeeper, Linda Carlton, is going to testify to shady business practices on Dad's part. Embezzlement, tax fraud—I'm not even sure about all the charges. The trial starts next Monday. I need to know if he's guilty of the charges against him."

Anna turned to Jessica, and their gazes held for several long moments. Jessica had told herself that she would be able to look into her mother's eyes and know for certain whether she was mentally and emotionally stable. She had been so certain that was all it would take. But now she wondered....

Anna certainly seemed rational enough, and her story was believable to anyone who knew Walter as well as Jessica did. But there were still several significant details that hadn't been explained—and the most obvious was sitting in a chair right next to Anna.

"We were on the yacht," Anna said. "Walter wanted to hold a big party for all his senior staff and business associates. His partner, Jeremy Carlton, was invited, of course, along with Jeremy's wife, Marla, and Marla's younger brother, Derek."

She explained that she had known Walter and Jeremy hadn't been getting along for some time. She had even overheard Walter threatening Jeremy in private, though they were cordial enough in public. She had also suspected that Walter was having an affair with Jeremy's wife—a suspicion that had turned out to be true, since twin boys, Tyler and Conrad, had been conceived from that affair.

"I knew it would be a miserable cruise, and I dreaded it. I turned to my usual solace," Anna added flatly. "I wasn't sober that evening, and my behavior was hardly exemplary. I flirted shamelessly with Derek, who was several years younger, and I made him fall for me. I seduced him to bolster my own battered ego. Later, I passed out cold."

Jessica glanced surreptitiously at Benton, who had said nothing since Anna began her story. She assumed that he had heard it before, since he showed no surprise at anything Anna revealed.

"It was while Derek was trying to revive me that he saw Walter throw Jeremy's body off the side of the yacht. Walter thought I was sleeping, and he believed everyone else had left the yacht. He wasn't worried about me being a witness—he was too confident that he could control me with threats about our children."

Jessica said, "Derek told me that he was too frightened to say anything about what he had seen. He had been drinking, and he was guilty of making love with Walter's wife. He didn't think anyone would believe him, and he was terrified that he would end up the same way as Jeremy if he tried to do anything."

Anna nodded in response to Jessica's comments. "He told me the same things later that night when he whispered to me what he had seen. He managed to smuggle me off the yacht and to his apartment, but then he didn't know what to do. He believed Walter would kill us both if he found out the truth. I believed the same. After all, Walter had gotten rid of Jeremy when his partner became an inconvenience. I suspect Jeremy had learned something about Walter's illegal business practices, and did not approve. And who were we to be believed against a man like Walter? His crazy wife? A callow boy in love?

"I convinced Derek to take me home and then leave town. And I was the one who suggested that he change his name and forget he'd ever met me or Walter."

Chapter Twelve

"You disapprove, Mr. Fields," Anna remarked, seeming not to mind whatever she had read in his expression. "I don't blame you. What Derek and I did was wrong, and a man got away with murder because of it—at least for twenty-five years.

"Walter concocted a story of how Jeremy had gotten drunk and fallen overboard, and without witnesses, the authorities had to accept that story despite their suspicions to the contrary. His wealth and power probably kept them from looking as closely at the facts as they might have otherwise. He always liked to boast that with enough wealth and connections, a man was above the laws that governed ordinary people."

"What happened then?" Jessica asked.

"I could not bear to look at Walter from that night on,

or to have him touch me. I spiraled into such a deep depression that I couldn't even get out of bed. Walter had no trouble convincing anyone that I needed to be institutionalized. Maybe he was even right at the beginning. But there was no reason for him to send me this far, or to keep me here for so long. He chose to lock me up and forget about me, and to make sure everyone else forgot me, too. It was four weeks after the night Jeremy Carlton died that I was shipped here."

"How did he keep you here against your will?"

"With money, Mr. Fields. A great deal of money. This place is lovely, and the residents are treated well, but we have no freedom. No choice in our own affairs. Someone else's money ensures that we stay here quietly out of the way. Most of the residents have suffered emotional problems in the past, and some truly need to be here. The rest of us simply became an embarrassment to our families."

"You never tried to get away? Never tried to contact attorneys or doctors in the States who could testify that you shouldn't be locked away?"

"A month after I arrived, I realized I was pregnant. I was just beginning to emerge from the paralyzing depression and I wanted very much to return to my children. But Walter made sure I got the message that I would not be welcomed at home. That he had made sure my reputation was so badly damaged that no judge would award me custody of my children. He even conveyed vague threats against my safety if I tried to return against his will."

She caught her breath. "I knew then that I had lost

my babies, as a result of his corruptness and my own weakness. I could not risk having him find out about my pregnancy—which I knew had to be a result of my night with Derek Ross. Walter would have insisted that my baby be destroyed, or taken away from me forever. I would not allow that.

"I had made some friends here, most notably a young doctor, Georges Rouiller. Dr. Rouiller was new to the staff, and had little influence with the management, but he was able to help me find someone to raise my child. He was a little in love with me then, I think, even though he was married and he knew we could never be together," she added with a hint of the vanity she had alluded to before. "He has been my friend and my supporter ever since. It wasn't that difficult for us to conceal the pregnancy from Walter, since he never called to ask about my welfare after he deposited me here."

"You stayed for Benton," Jessica murmured, looking from her mother to her newly discovered brother.

"Yes," Anna whispered. "It wasn't that I loved him any more than the four children I had left behind. Nor that I didn't long to be with you and your sister and brothers, Jessica. But you were lost to me, and Benton was all I had left. I simply couldn't take the risk.

"I was thrilled when I received that first letter from you nine years ago. I was afraid, of course, for you and for myself if Walter found out, but I had to know that you were all well. It has broken my heart that your father has turned the others against me so badly that they have had no interest in contacting me. And I was so sorry about what happened to you when you tried to come to me."

Jessica shrugged, taking on that faux-tough expression Sam recognized so well now. "I survived."

Her gruff tone hurt Sam's heart, because he knew how Jessica had suffered during the past few years. It couldn't be easy to find out the mother she had risked so much to contact and to try to visit had made little effort on her own behalf to be reunited with her eldest children.

"I became rather obsessed with protecting Benton from Walter," Anna admitted. "I was so sure Walter would harm him, perhaps because of the guilt I carried for leaving my other children, and for letting Walter get away with so many terrible things. Georges brought Marie Bressoux to me. A few years older than I, she was a wealthy widow with no children of her own. Georges' maternal aunt, actually. We made an arrangement whereby Marie would raise Benton as her own, giving him the best education and upbringing. Once a month, she brought him to see me. We told him that I was his aunt because we didn't want to confuse him."

"I figured out the truth by the time I was ten," Benton said. "They didn't lie to me when I asked them to confirm my guess."

"Benton was a brilliant child," Anna said with glowing pride. "He skipped several grades in school and finished university by the time he was eighteen. For the past five years, he has been working in the banking industry in Geneva, and already he is a very influential man."

"Mother tends to boast when it comes to me," Benton said indulgently. "She and Maman—which is what I call Marie Bressoux—still get together once a month just to discuss how wonderful I am. It's no surprise that I have a very healthy ego."

"Were you angry when you found out the truth?"

Benton looked a bit surprised by Jessica's question. "Why would I be angry? I was raised with the unconditional love and incredible support of two very special women. My childhood was a happy one."

Sam rested a hand on Jessica's knee, resenting for her sake that she couldn't make the same claim. "You know your mother doesn't belong in this place," he said to Benton, hearing the accusation in his own voice. "Why haven't you tried to get her out?"

"He could have done so, perhaps," Anna acknowledged for him. "But I asked him to leave things be. He needed to concentrate on building his own future. Walter left me alone as long as all that was required from him was a monthly check to the institution. When I heard from my daughter that she and my other children were well, I was able to stop worrying about them so much. Benton visits me often, as does Marie. They make sure I have everything I desire. I always knew that someday it would be safe to go home again, probably when Walter was dead. But having him in prison will be just as satisfactory," she added.

Sam had to wonder how Jessica felt at hearing the loathing in Anna's tone when she spoke of her husband. "Are you saying you're ready to go home now?" he asked.

Anna nodded. "I have been contacted about whether I would be willing to serve as a witness in Walter's trial.

Though I was, and am still concerned that my testimony would be twisted as that of a vengeful and unstable scorned wife, I am willing to do so."

Jessica moistened her lips. "You're going to testify against him?"

Anna's voice softened. "I'm going to tell the truth, darling. It's something I should have done twenty-five years ago."

"For what it's worth, he has been trying to make some amends," Jessica murmured. "He's made overtures to a couple of us since his arrest, and he even tried to apologize to me for some of the things he's done, though he doesn't do apologies very well."

"I hope his words bring some peace to you. But he will never be able to make amends to me for taking me away from my babies and depriving me of their childhoods."

"How do you plan to get back to California?" Sam asked, subtly changing the topic.

"My daughter bought an airline ticket for me when she purchased her own. I sent word through Derek that we would arrange the details of my release once she arrived here."

"I assumed I would be smuggling her out on my own somehow," Jessica added. "I didn't know about Benton, of course. I trust you will help me get her out of here?"

Benton nodded in confirmation.

Sam looked at Jessica. "You knew all along that you intended to take your mother home with you."

"Yes. I kept it a secret from everyone but Derek because I didn't want my father to get a hint of our plans."

She hadn't given *him* a hint, either, Sam couldn't

help thinking. She hadn't trusted him enough to tell him all her plans.

"I have to go back to make things right," Anna said. "And I want to see my other children. I want Benton to meet his other siblings, including Derek's daughter. And I want him to meet his father. I've been a coward for too long, hidden away here without fighting back. But my family needs me now. It's time for me to go home."

Sam hadn't said three words since they'd left the institution just over an hour earlier. Sitting on the side of the neatly made bed in their hotel room, Jessica watched from beneath her lashes as he paced, his thoughts hidden behind a stern expression.

"Are you angry with me?"

"You mean because you didn't tell me you were planning to take your mother home with you? Because you didn't trust me with that little tidbit?"

"It wasn't just you…" she began lamely.

"Oh, right. You didn't trust your father, either. Nice of you to put me in the same category with him."

"Give me a break, Sam. Only a few days ago you were working for him."

"And since then I've been totally on your side. Damn it, Jessica, we made love this morning. Doesn't that mean anything to you?"

She blinked. She had gotten the distinct impression that Sam had been the one who'd been unnerved by how close they'd gotten that morning. He had given off unmistakable "nervous bachelor" vibes afterward, and she had told herself it didn't matter because she didn't have any long-term plans for them, anyway. She knew exactly what that morning had been about, and a happily-ever-after ending wasn't a part of it. "I, um—"

"Never mind. What time are you supposed to meet your brother for dinner?"

"We have another hour. You're invited, too, you know. Benton made that very clear."

Sam shook his head. "You should take this chance to get to know him better and to finalize your plans for springing your mother tomorrow. I'll entertain myself."

"Are you sure?"

"Yes." He turned to pace the other direction.

Perched on the very edge of the mattress with her fingers tucked beneath her, Jessica continued to watch him. "What did you think about my mother? About the things she told us?"

Reaching up to massage the back of his neck, he glanced her way. "Are you asking if I think she's sane?"

"Just your general impressions of her. Honestly."

He shrugged. "Honestly? I think she's more than a little self-centered, vain, overly dramatic and probably a bit paranoid. I doubt that she'll ever be named mother of the year, but she seems like a nice enough woman, on the whole. She's made some very poor decisions in the past, but she's had to pay more severely for them than she should have. And I think she's as sane as most people. There's no reason at all for her to remain locked up."

She had asked for his honest opinion, she reminded herself when she felt tempted to protest his somewhat unflattering assessment of her mother's character. And to be truthful, he was probably right on target with much of it. But at least he didn't think she was crazy.

"So what do you think will happen when you take her home?" he asked. "How are your other siblings going to feel about her showing up so belatedly to testify against your father?"

"Once they hear her story, I'm sure they'll accept her the same way I have."

"And Benton? How will they accept him?"

"The same way they have our other newly found brothers, I suppose. Pragmatically. And as for whatever happens in court, I'm sure as long as Mother tells the truth, justice will be done."

"You trust her to tell the truth? She hates your father, you know."

"I know. But I'll have to trust the attorneys and the jury to sort out truth from bitterness and anger."

He nodded. "If she's as honest about her own mistakes as she was with us today, there's no reason to doubt her story. And she seems determined enough to stick with it, no matter how unpleasant it becomes for her."

She was relieved to hear that. She had wondered if Anna would be able to bear up under the charges of insanity and revenge that Walter's attorneys would most likely throw at her.

"The tabloids are going to love finding out there's yet another illegitimate member of my family."

"Forget the tabloids. Something new will catch their interest soon enough. Besides, maybe the notoriety will help you sell more of your paintings."

"Cynical way to look at it, but maybe you're right."

"Hey, if you can't beat them, use them to your advantage." Sam glanced at his watch then. "I think I'll head on out and let you get dressed for your dinner. I'll let myself in with my key when I return. Don't worry if it's late. There are a few old haunts I might visit."

She lifted her chin. "Fine. Have a good time."

"Yeah. You, too."

She glared at the door after he closed it behind him on his way out. She would never understand that man and the way he changed from one moment to the next.

Maybe that was his intention. Maybe his ex-wife had hurt him so badly that he would never let anyone get too close to him again. A woman could break her heart trying—and Jessica had already spent too much of her life chasing after impossible dreams.

Jessica had left the bathroom light on and the bathroom door partially ajar when she went to bed that night because she didn't want to lie alone in the dark. Still, she doubted that Sam could see that she was awake when he tiptoed into the room sometime after midnight.

From where she lay on the pillows, she watched him lock the door behind himself, then move stealthily toward the sofa, stripping off his jacket on the way. "Did you have a good time?"

Her voice made him freeze. "Sorry. Did I wake you?"

"No. I wasn't asleep."

"Oh." Silhouetted against the light from the bathroom, he sat on the sofa and took off his shoes. "Did you have a nice dinner with your brother?"

"Yes, very nice. He's an interesting man."

"Yeah, I got that impression."

"You didn't like him?"

"I didn't say that."

She silently watched him remove his shirt.

"Good thing we're going home tomorrow," he murmured. "I'd have had to buy some clothes."

At the reminder that their time together was coming to an end, Jessica clutched the sheet more tightly to her chin. "What are you going to do when we get back? Do you have any more clients lined up?"

"A few."

He wasn't in a very talkative mood, apparently. She supposed he was tired from his evening of…whatever he had been doing for the hours he'd been gone. "So, did you have a good time tonight?"

"Shouldn't you be getting some sleep? You've got a big day ahead of you tomorrow."

She bit her lower lip and remained quiet while he went into the bathroom and closed the door behind him, plunging the room into darkness. She regretted the distance between them, but maybe it was better to end things sooner rather than later. He obviously regretted making love with her, and he was sending her the message that there would be nothing more between them once they returned to California.

She told herself that was fine with her. She had a lot going on in her life. She didn't need any more complications. She didn't need Sam Fields.

Whether she still wanted him—well, that was a different issue.

The bathroom door opened again. "You want me to leave this light on?"

"No, you can turn it off."

A moment later the light was gone. She heard him move, and she wondered again how he made his way so well in the dark.

A solid, painful-sounding thud made her wince even as Sam let out a string of muttered curses. She sat up and reached for the lamp beside the bed. The light showed Sam clad only in dark boxer shorts as he leaned over to massage the shin he'd cracked against the coffee table.

"Sorry," he said. "I'm okay."

"Are you sure you're all right?"

"It's just a bruise."

"It sounded as though you hit it pretty hard."

"I'm fine, Jessica. Go to sleep, okay?"

She looked at him, standing there so bare and so gorgeously male. "I'm not sure I can."

What might have been a groan escaped him. "I'm giving you fair warning. Turn off the light and go to sleep or I'm joining you in that bed. I'm not made out of stone, Jessica."

"Neither am I."

"It's probably not a good idea," he said, though he took a step toward the bed even as he spoke. "Everything in your life is so chaotic right now, it's got to be hard for you to think clearly."

"Are you saying I'm crazy?" she asked politely.

"God, no." He sounded appalled.

"Because you would probably be right. Maybe it's

unwise, but I don't care right now. I don't want you to sleep on that couch tonight."

He put one knee on the mattress beside her. "I don't think I'd get much sleep over there even if I tried."

Reaching up to pull him down to her, she smiled against his mouth. "I wouldn't bet on getting much sleep here, either."

He seemed to have no complaints.

Chapter Thirteen

Sam watched Switzerland slowly disappear below him as the airplane climbed above a bank of thick, white clouds. He sat in the window seat with Jessica on his right. Anna sat in the aisle seat.

He would have offered Jessica his hand during take-off, but it hadn't been necessary. She had clung, instead, to her mother. She'd barely looked away from her mother ever since Benton had delivered Anna to the Geneva airport two takeoffs ago.

Sam didn't know quite how Benton had arranged Anna's release, though he suspected money and the mysterious Dr. Rouiller were involved.

Benton had said he couldn't get away from work just now, but that he would come to San Francisco as soon as he could to meet his father and his other half siblings.

He had hugged his mother tightly at the airport and then asked Sam to take care of both Anna and Jessica—a request Jessica had gotten a bit chippy about, since she was so into taking care of herself these days.

Sam was trying hard not to mind that Jessica had practically forgotten his existence since Anna had joined them. It was only natural, he told himself, that she would be absorbed with her long-lost mother after longing for so many years to meet her. They had a lot to catch up on, and the way they were chattering, they were going to try to learn everything there was to know about each other during this flight. Sam might as well pull out a book or something.

Of course, it did seem as if a woman would pay just a little attention to the man who had spent most of the night making passionate love to her, he thought with a scowl.

She did try once or twice to include him in the conversation, but her efforts didn't get them very far. Anna seemed to have little interest in talking to him. Whether she still didn't trust him because he had worked for her husband, or whether she sensed undercurrents between him and her daughter that made her uncomfortable, Sam couldn't say, but her attitude was decidedly cool toward him. Jessica gave him an occasional, faintly apologetic look, but he merely shrugged to indicate that he understood. Mostly.

He wondered if this was the way all the Parks would treat him if he tried to socialize with them. Walter would have no use for him after this, of course, and he would be livid if he knew just how close Sam and Jessica had become on this trip he had futilely tried to prevent. Sam figured he'd be lucky not to end up like the late Jeremy Carlton.

But what about her siblings? How would they feel about the ex-cop-turned-P.I. who had basically stalked and then seduced their sister? At least, that was probably the way they would see it.

He didn't try to delude himself that he was their social equal. Blue collar all the way, that was his background. Father a beat cop and a drunk, mother a struggling immigrant. Half his own family hadn't wanted anything to do with him.

Even with the current scandal, the Parks moved among San Francisco's elite. Emily Parks had married a friggin' king. Sam doubted that he would be seen as a suitable match for the youngest Parks daughter.

Not that he was considering marriage, of course. He wasn't in any hurry to make that mistake again. He was just imagining what would happen if he were even to hint at such a union to members of Jessica's highbrow family.

Jessica finally turned to him when Anna dozed off halfway through the flight. "She's so excited she's worn herself out," Jessica murmured.

"Or maybe she's worn herself out talking," Sam replied with a smile that felt fake. "Guess the two of you had a lot to discuss."

"She wanted to hear everything about my brothers and sister and everything we've all been up to for the past twenty-five years. She's missed so much in our lives."

He had to concede the truth of that. "It was very cruel of your father to take her away from her children."

"He'll never be able to justify that to me," she replied with quiet intensity. "Never."

"There is no justification."

She touched his hand where it rested on the armrest. "Sam?"

Just that light contact had made his heart beat a little faster. Someone who didn't know him better might even think he was lovesick, he thought ruefully. "Yes?"

"Thank you for helping me bring my mother home."

"You're welcome."

She rested her cheek against his shoulder in a gesture that held so much trust it made his chest tighten. "I can't get over how much you sacrificed for me. Dad will never pay you for this, of course. And if he manages to get the word out, he could harm your reputation with your other clients."

"Well, um, I was paid in advance for coming on this trip," he admitted candidly. "Your father transferred some cash into my bank account with a couple of phone calls from jail. He can't get it back now, no matter how furious he gets."

She lifted her head. "Oh. I didn't realize…."

"As for my reputation, I think his is a bit more tarnished at the moment. I'm not too concerned about anything he might have to say to my potential clients."

"Well. Good." She smiled very brightly. "I'm glad you didn't really have anything to lose by switching allegiance."

He wouldn't say that, exactly. He'd been very close

to losing his heart. Good thing he hadn't let it go quite that far, he assured himself.

"So what's the plan when you get back to San Francisco? Are you taking your mother straight back to the estate?"

"Yes. I'll call Cade from the airport and tell him we're on our way. What about you?"

"I'll need to check in at my office, of course. I have a new associate who's been keeping things going in my absence, but I'm sure I'll have a stack of things to take care of."

"A new associate?"

"Mmm. You met him once, actually. In a coffee shop near your bank. He told me you recommended a mocha latte to him."

She grimaced as she obviously remembered the exchange. "I just knew there was something about him…and I thought I was being paranoid again," she added rather accusingly.

"Sorry. You'd gotten too good at spotting me. I had to send someone else."

He wasn't sure why he'd told her. Maybe to remind both of them just who he was and where he'd fit into her life before. Nowhere, actually.

"He's a nice guy," he added lamely. "His name is Ed and he's a retired cop. A widower who needed something to fill his days."

"So you hired him. That's very generous of you."

Sam shrugged. "I needed the help."

"Yes, of course. Watching me was taking up so much of your valuable time."

"Jessica—"

Anna stirred, and Jessica turned immediately back to her mother.

Sam subsided glumly against the window. Okay, that conversation hadn't gone very well.

It was going to be a very long trip home.

Jessica noticed that Sam had his cell phone to his ear almost the moment they stepped off the plane at the airport. She assumed he was calling his office. She placed a quick call to Cade, who seemed relieved that she was back safely and agreed to meet her at the estate in a couple of hours. She didn't tell him who she had with her. She then placed a quick call to Caroline, leaving a message on her machine that she was back in town and would see her soon.

Those were the only people who might have genuinely worried about her while she was away, she mused, ending the second call.

"It feels so strange to be surrounded by so many people," Anna murmured, looking rather dazedly around the crowded airport. "It's been so long…."

Jessica took her mother's arm. "I'm sure there will be a period of adjustment for you," she said sympathetically. "Twenty-five years is a long time to spend strictly in one environment."

Anna's smile was a bit shaky. "So I keep telling myself whenever I find myself almost wishing to be back in the security of my rooms."

Jessica remembered how disorienting it had been for her to be returned to her family and her regular routines after being held for only two weeks by her kidnappers. She could imagine how Anna felt now. "You look a little pale. Why don't I get you a bottled water or something?"

Anna nodded. "Yes, I think I could use that."

Jessica looked at Sam, who had put away his phone and returned to where she and Anna stood. "Would you mind helping my mother find a seat? I'm going to get her some water. She just needs a minute to get her bearings."

"Of course." Despite the rather cool way Anna had treated him, Sam was nothing but solicitous when he offered her his arm. "I see an empty bench right over there, Mrs. Parks. Let me help you."

With the air of a woman who simply couldn't resist an attractive man's attentions, Anna reached out to rest her fingertips lightly on his arm, her smile holding just a shade of regal condescension. Anna might have spent the past twenty-five years in seclusion, but there were certain things she remembered quite well, Jessica thought with wry amusement.

Moving toward a counter where soft drinks and bottled water were sold, she felt the weariness of the long trip making her steps drag a bit. It was almost 6:00 p.m. here in California, nine hours earlier than Switzerland. She'd been up since the crack of dawn, Swiss time, after a night of interrupted sleep. She could use a solid eight hours of unconsciousness.

Not that she was complaining about her lack of sleep last night, she thought with a reminiscent smile. But then that smile faded as she found herself wondering if she would ever spend another night in Sam's arms.

* * *

Anna Parks was a woman who was accustomed to being catered to, Sam couldn't help noticing. Maybe she had spent half her life in an institution, but she'd apparently been treated like royalty there, judging from the way she acted with him.

"There's a wet wipe in the outside pocket of my bag," she said, waving a hand toward the leather tote sitting some six inches from her on the bench. "I saved it from the plane. Perhaps you could get it for me so I can wipe my face?"

"Of course." His mouth twisting a bit, Sam fished out the packet and opened it for her, unfolding the wipe before offering it to her.

"Thank you." She touched the dampened, lemon-scented square of paper delicately to her throat and forehead.

"I know that was a long, hard journey for you," Sam said, trying to sound sympathetic.

Dropping both the towelette and the queenly manner, Anna frowned at him. "I am not an old woman, Mr. Fields."

No. She was only twelve years his senior, actually. The same difference as between himself and Jessica, Sam thought with a slight wince. "I'm sorry. I didn't mean to imply that you are."

She sighed a little, and turned to toss the wipe into a nearby trash can. "I'm afraid I haven't been very polite to you. It's hard to get past the fact that you worked for Walter."

"I understand. Your daughter felt the same way about

me at first." He wasn't entirely sure that Jessica had ever completely gotten over it, either. The closer they'd come to California, the more she'd seemed to pull back from him.

He couldn't help wondering if he was just another check mark on the list of things she had done to defy her father during the past few days.

"Are you in love with my daughter, Mr. Fields?"

Just where *was* Jessica, anyway? He glanced toward the counter toward which she'd been headed, but a crowd of Japanese tourists were milling between there and where he stood, blocking his view. "Um—"

"Feel free to tell me it's none of my business. I merely wanted to see your expression when I asked."

"It's none of your business. And your daughter is very much like you, Mrs. Parks. Both of you have a way of making my head spin."

She seemed to like that. "You have potential, Mr. Fields."

He smiled. "So do you, Mrs. Parks."

"Anna."

"Sam."

She nodded, then looked across the terminal. "It's taking Jessica a while. Is there a long line?"

The tour group had moved on now, and Sam stood to get a better view of the refreshments counter. He frowned when he didn't see Jessica there—or anywhere else in the vicinity.

"Maybe she went to the ladies' room," Anna suggested, looking in the same direction.

"Maybe." Although he would have expected her to

tell him where she was going, it was just like Jessica to pop out of sight without thinking that it would make him nervous.

Anna stood. "Why don't I go in and see? I'm sure she's just freshening up from the trip."

Sam supposed his urge to yell at Jessica was an over-reaction. He wasn't her bodyguard anymore; there was no need for him to be.

Ten minutes later, he had reason to regret giving up his responsibilities so soon.

Jessica was missing.

Jessica had been angry with her father before, but never to this extent. If she hadn't known how closely they were being watched by his guards, she would have thrown herself at him in a genuine effort to throttle him.

"How *dare* you have some goon snatch me from the airport!" she raged at him, strangled fury more than discretion keeping her voice low. "How dare you have me brought here against my will? What gives you the right to frighten me like that again? What kind of monster are you?"

Walter Parks looked more like a haggard old man than a monster at that moment, but that was beside the point as far as she was concerned. She wouldn't allow herself to be concerned with how much he had aged here, not when he was still acting like the same arrogant, overly controlling, heartless man she knew all too well.

Facing her from the other side of a table in the tiny visitation room—one Jessica suspected was usually re-served for attorneys and their clients—Walter held up a hand to silence her. "There's no need for melodrama, Jessica. I know you're angry with me, but it was the only way I could get you to come to me. I've asked you to visit me before, and you refused."

"So you had me kidnapped? How did you know I was at the airport, anyway?"

"I've had a man stationed at the airport for a couple of days. I asked someone to notify him as soon as you returned from your trip, and he took it from there."

She flashed to a mental picture of Sam talking on his cell phone so quickly after they'd stepped off the plane. Surely he hadn't—

Walter went on before she could complete that sickening thought. "I'm sorry you were frightened. I instructed my man to reassure you as soon as you recovered sufficiently to understand where he was bringing you."

"Oh, I knew who was behind it as soon as my head cleared while I was in the car on the way here. What was that he sprayed me with, anyway? My whole mind blanked out until I couldn't even form a coherent thought. I still have a vicious headache."

"I'm sorry. It was just a little something to make you dizzy and disoriented so my man could escort you out of the airport with the excuse that you were ill and needed fresh air. No one questioned him, since you looked so pale and sick. I've been assured that it leaves no lasting effects—other than the headache, I'm afraid."

"Yeah, I'm sure that means a lot to you," she muttered, rubbing her temples. "You bastard."

She had never in her life spoken to him that way, no matter how defiant she had been at times. And it felt good.

It was a measure of his control that he didn't lose his temper, though a wave of red darkened his throat in a sign of anger. "I simply wanted to talk to you, Jessica. I knew you wouldn't come on your own."

"And you've never been overly concerned with giving other people a choice about something you want, have you? I don't know why you want to talk to me, anyway. I've already been to Switzerland. It's certainly too late to stop me now."

"I know you were somehow able to get in to see your mother in the asylum. I want to know what she said to you while you were there. And I want to know how much she convinced you to believe."

Jessica lifted an eyebrow. "Is it possible your source didn't tell you everything?"

"What are you talking about?"

"I brought Mother home with me. And if you make any effort whatever to harm her, I'll see that you fry. Is that perfectly clear?"

The flush of anger receded, leaving Walter pasty pale. "You brought her back with you? That's impossible."

"Is it?"

"She couldn't be released from the institution. I have paperwork."

Her laugh was bitter. "Your 'paperwork' isn't worth the paper it's written on. Turns out Mother has some connections in Switzerland that are just as powerful as you are. She's merely been waiting for the right time to use them to secure her release."

Walter clutched at his chest. "You would do this to me? Your own father."

Her lip curled. "Now who's being melodramatic? Give it up, Dad. You gave it your best shot and you lost. I'm free of you now—and so is my mother."

"She'll destroy me with her lies."

"If you are destroyed, it was your own doing, not hers."

Walter shook his head sadly. "I have always loved you and tried to protect you, Jessica. I love all my children. But what you've done—I can't protect you anymore. You'll all have to live with the shame and the scandal. And you'll have to bear the heartache when your mother turns on you the way she did me. When she abandons you as she did before."

Jessica stood then, and leaned against the table, supporting herself on her hands. The guard in the corner had gone on alert, moving a bit closer to her, but she ignored him. "I don't want to hear you say anything more about her. Yes, she's flawed—as we all are. But she didn't deserve what you did to her. None of us did."

"I just hope you don't live to regret what you've done."

Straightening, Jessica continued to hold his gaze with her own. "You can't scare me anymore, Dad. I can deal with the repercussions of any mistakes I might make on my own. We all have to pay for our actions at some point. You're paying for yours now."

One hand still resting on his chest, Walter was silent for a long moment. When he spoke, there was defeat in his voice for the first time Jessica could remember. "I've lost any love you've felt for me, haven't I?"

Her eyes filled then, despite her efforts to hold back the tears. Her own voice shook. "You didn't lose my love, Dad. You threw it away a long time ago."

Swallowing a sob, she turned toward the door then. "I want to go home."

"My man will drive you. He's been instructed to take you wherever you want to go."

"Goodbye, Dad."

When the guard held the door for her, she walked out without looking back.

It was dark now, but the prison parking lot was so brightly illuminated it could have been noon. Sam spotted Jessica as she stepped out of the prison door, escorted by a rather hulking sort who followed respectfully behind her. Having run that far from his car, Sam slowed a bit to catch his breath—the first time he had taken a full breath since he'd realized Jessica was missing from the airport.

"Thank God," he said.

She must have heard him, even above the bustle of the people coming and going around them. She turned her head and met his eyes. It hurt his heart when her expression didn't change. There was no pleasure to see him in her eyes, no relief. Nothing except a dull, weary pain.

"What a surprise for you to show up here," she said tonelessly.

He resisted an impulse to catch her in his arms only because he suspected she would have pushed him away. She had to be on emotional overload, so he would try to put aside his own need to just touch her and assure himself she was safe. "Damn, I'm glad you're here. I hoped I wasn't wrong about my guess about where you'd been taken."

"Brilliant deduction." She sounded oddly mocking. "Where's my mother?"

"I stashed her at my place with my associate, Ed. He agreed to keep her safe until I brought you back to her. She was very upset when you disappeared, but I convinced her I would find you. Last I saw, she was being consoled by Ed, who looked thoroughly smitten with her."

"You must have been confident you knew where I was."

"As I said, I guessed that if Walter hadn't brought you here, he'd know where you were. I was going to choke it out of him if necessary."

"Mmm." Jessica glanced at the man who lurked behind her. Her voice was cold when she spoke. "You can go. Mr. Fields will take me to my mother."

The man hesitated until Sam gave him a dismissive scowl. And then he nodded and moved away.

Jessica's expression was no warmer when she turned back to Sam. "Where's your car?"

"This way." He reached out automatically to place a hand at her back. She moved immediately away from his touch, making him drop his hand to his side.

Either she was still in shock, or she was just mad at the world in general, Sam figured. He couldn't really blame her for either.

He didn't know what he had done specifically to annoy her, unless it was letting down his guard at the airport so that she was snatched away right out from under his nose. She couldn't be angrier about that than he was at himself.

He still couldn't think about the moment he had realized she was gone without breaking into a cold sweat.

He'd wanted to head straight to Walter Parks right then, but he'd had her semihysterical mother to deal with. He'd kept his composure while he'd taken care of her, but inside he'd been a mess.

If he had been wrong about Walter being behind Jessica's disappearance…

"What happened at the airport?" he asked when they were belted into his SUV.

She told him in as few words as possible about the hand that had suddenly appeared in front of her, and the noxious spray that had clouded her mind and made it so easy for the man to "assist" her to his car.

Belatedly putting two and two together, Sam cursed beneath his breath, his hands clenching on the steering wheel. "It was that guy? The one who followed you out to the parking lot?"

"Yes. Dad's 'man.'"

"Damn it, if I'd known what he did to you, I'd have bashed his face in."

"That isn't necessary."

Maybe not, but it would have made *him* feel better, Sam fumed. Since he couldn't beat up Walter for scaring the hell out of everyone with this stunt, it would have felt pretty damn good to take his frustration out on Walter's representative.

"How could he have known you were going to be there at that time?"

"Dad said someone notified him as soon as we landed."

"Who…?"

Something about the look she gave him then stopped his words in his throat. "Surely you don't think…?"

She turned her head to look out the window. Sam was forcibly reminded of the first time they had left the asylum, when she had all but accused him of scheming in French with Chantal to keep Jessica away from her mother.

He felt his temper rising, and considering what he had been through during that very long day, he wasn't entirely sure of his ability to keep it from boiling over. "I called my office. Ed doesn't know your father, and he didn't call him."

And rather than give her a chance to express further doubts about him, he slammed one fist against the steering wheel. "Damn it, I'm tired of trying to prove myself to you! Have I been nothing more to you than another reckless adventure aimed at hitting your father where it hurts most? Someone you can't really trust, but don't mind using, is that it? What more do you want me to do for you, Jessica?"

"Could you please just take me to my mother?" she whispered.

"Isn't that what I've been doing all along?" he responded bitterly.

She didn't answer.

Chapter Fourteen

An emotional reunion with her mother pretty much put an end to any chance at further conversation between Jessica and Sam. He stood quietly in the background while Jessica described the enforced meeting with Walter to her irate mother.

"I'll see that he pays for that," Anna said between clenched teeth.

"Just tell the truth about whatever happened, Mother," Jessica answered wearily. "He'll get whatever justice he deserves if everyone just tells the truth."

"My poor darling, you're dead on your feet." Anna looked at Sam. "Would you mind taking us home so we can get some rest?"

"Ed's going to drive you to the estate," Sam replied. "I have some things to catch up on here."

"Here" was his home—a small house furnished in what Jessica thought of as "modern bachelor" style. Top of the line electronics, and a minimum of furniture and decorations. She hadn't really had a chance to look around, but she had seen little of his personality in the one room she'd been in, the living room.

Anna smiled at Ed. "That's very kind of you."

The gruff-natured ex-cop cleared his throat and shifted self-consciously on his feet. "No trouble, ma'am."

Jessica knew they should be on their way. She had called Cade and explained the delay to him. Waiting until he had calmed down enough to listen to her again, she made him promise not to leave the estate until she arrived.

She would have to make arrangements to retrieve her car from the Oakland airport. And heaven only knew what had happened to her bags. She didn't know if Sam and Anna had waited long enough to retrieve luggage before going in search of her, but at the moment she just didn't care. She was so very tired.

Ed gestured toward the door, offering to escort them out. Jessica looked at Sam, trying to decide what to say.

He didn't give her much chance to say anything. "You know where to find me if you need me."

Thinking it sounded very much like a brush-off, she nodded. "Good night, Sam."

There was no emotion on his face, but his eyes were dark with them when he looked back at her, his hands stuck in the pockets of his jeans. "Goodbye, Jessica."

She had thought she was too tired to even feel hurt. She had been wrong.

* * *

It was the most unusual Thanksgiving dinner Jessica had ever experienced. Her mother was there, for the first time in Jessica's memory. And her brothers were both accompanied by new spouses this year. Emily was absent, tied by royal duties in her new husband's country, though she had called that morning and promised to be home for Christmas. Benton would also be arriving just before Christmas, giving him a chance to meet all his half siblings at one time.

Anna was thriving on being reunited with her family. Sitting at the head of the table like a queen bee, she beamed at them all. Initial awkwardness was fading as they all spent more time together.

After hearing Anna's story, her children had all agreed to forgive her for the weaknesses that had led to her initial separation from them. They acknowledged that she'd had little say over what had happened to her since. All too familiar with their father's dictatorial behavior, they knew what it was like to be fully controlled by him.

For her part, Anna was delighted to find that her eldest children were happy and well. She immediately fell in love with Cade's adorably blond, five-year-old daughter, Stacy, though it still seemed a bit odd to her to hear herself called grandmother. And, while it had startled her to discover that Cade's new bride, Sara, was the daughter of Jeremy and Marla Carlton, she was soon won over by her daughter-in-law's pleasant nature. Not to mention Sara's obvious adoration of Cade.

The least demonstrative of the Parks offspring, Rowan had accepted his mother's homecoming with his usual equanimity. He, too, was a father now, having married Louanne Brown, the single mother of a precious one-year-old son, Noah. Jessica was actually surprised at how readily Rowan was adapting to his new role as husband and father. Falling in love had given him a new peace within himself that pleased his siblings, since he seemed truly content for the first time in their memory.

No mention was made of the most notably missing member of the family, though he was obviously present in everyone's mind.

Jessica couldn't help looking around at one point and thinking that an outsider looking in at them now would think they were a normal family. She had a fleeting moment of regret for the twenty-five years of separation from their mother, and for the father to whom wealth and power had meant more than family and honor. But it would do her no good to dwell on the past or fret about the future. She should concentrate, instead, on the present.

Not that the present was entirely rosy. The preliminary hearing to determine whether Walter would be tried for all of the charges against him, including the murder of Jeremy Carlton, would begin Monday, and that wasn't going to be easy for any of them.

And then there was Sam. Letting the others carry on the lively conversations around the table, Jessica pushed a piece of turkey around her plate with her fork and let herself drift into memories....

"Darling, are you all right? You look so pensive."

She forced a smile in response to her mother's concerned question. "I'm just enjoying our Thanksgiving together."

She knew the others were surreptitiously studying her face. Her siblings didn't know quite what to make of her since her return from Switzerland. They were all surprised she'd had the nerve to try anything like that again, and that she had managed to pull it off successfully.

Now that they knew Anna wasn't crazy, they could stop worrying so much about Jessica. But that meant they had to make a few adjustments in their thinking about her.

She was also aware that she had changed during that trip. She was no longer Walter Parks's anxious, reclusive, withdrawn youngest child. She had gone to Switzerland to find her mother, but in the process she had reclaimed herself. She had broken away from her fears, her ultrasafe routines, her father's domination.

And, though no one knew but her, she had fallen in love. Even if that love had left heartache behind, it was still a rite of passage she wouldn't have taken back even if she could.

But as she looked at her brothers sitting so happily around the Thanksgiving table with their new families, she couldn't help wishing....

Sam ate Thanksgiving dinner sitting in his recliner in front of a football game on the TV. His meal consisted of a thick turkey and provolone sandwich on whole wheat bread, a bag of jalapeño-flavored potato chips and a beer. He had a bakery pumpkin pie in the refrigerator for later.

Thanksgiving had never been much of an event in his past. Since his mother hadn't grown up with the tradition, she hadn't been overly attached to observing it. His father had seen it only as a day of football and booze. He and Janice hadn't been married long enough to form their own Thanksgiving rituals. As far as Sam was concerned, it was just another day.

But he couldn't help thinking that it must be much more than that for Jessica, especially this year. He could easily picture her sitting at a table with her family, so grateful to have their mother back among them. She was probably having such a good time that no thought of him even crossed her mind.

His appetite suddenly gone, he set the last couple bites of his sandwich aside and tried to muster some enthusiasm for the game.

Jessica stood in front of a canvas in her studio, studied the single stroke of red paint across it, and then set her brush down with a sigh. It was Saturday afternoon, and she had been trying to paint for the past three hours, this one red line all she had to show for her efforts.

For some reason she couldn't stop thinking about Sam. How could she miss him this badly when he had been in her life such a short time?

You know where to find me if you need me.

The memory of his words made her shiver. She wouldn't go so far as to say that she needed him, now that she had declared herself an independent woman who no longer relied on anyone but herself. But she had to concede that she wanted him.

She should be accustomed by now to not having everything she wanted.

Wandering out of the studio a few minutes later, she

went into her bedroom. She had spent the first couple of nights since arriving from Switzerland in the main house with her mother, but then she had returned to her own cottage. Anna seemed to be comfortably ensconced in the mansion again, but Jessica would never again feel that it was her home. There were too many painful memories for her there. She would always enjoy visiting her mother at the mansion, if that was where she chose to stay, but Jessica needed to find a place that was hers alone.

On an impulse, she opened the drawer of her dresser where she had stashed the small items she'd found in her possession during the weeks before her trip. She took them out of the drawer and arranged them on her bed, studying each one thoughtfully.

A knock on her front door made her straighten her shoulders and draw a deep breath before she moved to answer it. She wasn't looking forward to this visit, if her caller was who she expected.

Caroline Harper stood on the doorstep wearing designer clothes and a slightly puzzled smile. "I'm here, just as you requested," she announced unnecessarily.

"So I see. Come in."

Studying Jessica from the corner of her eyes, Caroline entered the living room and tossed her purse on a table. "It's really good to see you, Jess. You look great. How's your mother?"

"She's adjusting very well, thank you." Though Jessica hadn't seen Caroline since she'd returned, they'd had one long telephone conversation, during which Jessica had caught Caroline up on everything that had happened. Leaving out a few pertinent details, of course, mostly related to Sam.

It was only after that talk that Jessica had begun to think about all the times she and Caroline had been together in the past few months. And about a few other things that had been nagging at her since she'd returned from Switzerland, making only two calls from the airport.

"So, why did you want to see me so badly today? It's not that I didn't want to see you, you know that, it's just that it's sort of a hectic time for me."

Jessica motioned toward her bedroom door. "I'd like to show you something. If you wouldn't mind…?"

"Okay. Sure." Looking even more bemused now, Caroline entered the bedroom with Jessica close behind her. Caroline stopped abruptly when she saw the objects spread out on the bedspread. "What—?"

"I thought I was going crazy, you know," Jessica said conversationally. She moved to stand by the bed, picking up the clown-shaped refrigerator magnet. "I was terrified that my father would have me locked away."

"I don't know what…"

Caroline's denial faded into silence when Jessica looked up at her. "Please don't lie to me, Caroline. Not this time."

"Damn it." Apparently unable to look into Jessica's eyes, Caroline half turned away. "He convinced me it was for your own good."

"You thought it was good for me to think I was going insane?" Jessica was proud that her voice still sounded detached, unemotional.

"He said you were getting out of control. That you

were planning some crazy trip to Switzerland to break your crazy mother out of the institution. He said he was having you watched, but that he worried you would get away from him. He thought if little things started happening to make you doubt yourself, you'd be too frightened to try anything, giving him time to get help for you."

"How many 'little things' did you arrange for me?"

"A few. He might have had some other people doing things, too. I don't know for sure."

"You altered my paintings?"

"Yes. I was afraid that was carrying things a little too far."

Jessica might have laughed bitterly at that had it not hurt so badly. "He paid you."

Caroline hesitated only a moment before nodding. "I needed the money. My credit cards were maxed out and I was having trouble making the payments. It isn't cheap living in the style to which I would like to become accustomed, you know," she added with a characteristic attempt at sarcastic humor. "Not that you would know about that, having grown up on this luxurious estate with everything you ever wanted."

When Jessica didn't respond in any way to that, Caroline shrugged a little and went on, "I believed him, you know. He seemed so sincere when he talked to me. He was the very image of the concerned father—the one I always wished I'd had for myself. I believed your mother was insane, I believed your father was being framed for those crimes, and I believed that you were in trouble and wouldn't let anyone help you."

Jessica wasn't particularly swayed by Caroline's arguments. She suspected the money had a lot to do with making her usually shrewd and cynical friend more gullible than usual when it came to Walter's lies.

"You notified my father that I was back in town, didn't you?" she asked quietly. "I called you almost as soon as I touched down, and when you got the message, you relayed it to my father so he could have me snatched from the airport."

"I didn't know that was what he was going to do, of course," Caroline replied defensively. "I just assumed he wanted to make sure you were safe, maybe get you straight into counseling. And I didn't know your mother was with you. You didn't say on the message."

"It's a good thing I didn't mention her. He might have arranged to have her taken, too, had he known. And I'm not entirely sure she would have been safely returned. She's too much of a threat to him."

"You really think he's guilty of murder."

Jessica stepped squarely into Caroline's view. "I know he is," she said steadily. "He removed all doubt when he ordered someone to use a noxious spray on me and kidnap me from that airport. And I know that you're guilty of conspiring with a murderer to betray someone who thought of you as her only close friend."

"Jessica, I'm sorry. I didn't mean—"

"Please leave now."

Caroline hesitated only a moment before turning for the door. Jessica followed, this time to lock the door behind her former friend for the final time.

Caroline paused just inside the doorway, looking

back with an expression in her eyes that might have been genuine regret. "You've always known what I really was. You always seemed to like me, anyway."

"I did. Yet I mistakenly believed that I could trust you, as well. I never wanted you to be perfect, Caroline, but I needed you to be on my side. It turns out the only side you were on was your own. I can't be friends with someone who's just like my father."

Her face going pale, Caroline started to speak, but then simply turned and left.

There were tears in Jessica's eyes when she locked the door. And a hole in her heart that grew bigger every time someone else who had mattered to her walked away from her.

Sitting at the back of the crowded courtroom, Sam watched as Linda Mailer Carlton, Walter Parks's former accountant, placed one hand on a Bible, raised the other, then swore to tell the truth. The room grew silent as she began to testify, nervously toying with a small medallion that hung from a chain around her neck as she did so.

The mounting evidence being presented against Walter Parks was damning. Smuggling, embezzlement, tax fraud, murder. It was becoming very clear that Jeremy Carlton had begun to suspect that his partner was involved in illegal activities and had decided to quietly gather evidence against him. The prosecution claimed that Walter had been planning an offshore pickup of smuggled gems, and that Jeremy had hoped to catch him in that act. Walter had killed him rather than risk paying for his actions.

There were witnesses, and recently uncovered papers and financial books to back up the prosecution's charges. Marla Carlton had told her children everything just before she died, including that her brother, Derek, knew the truth, if they could find him and convince him to talk.

The defense team had an increasingly difficult, if not impossible, task ahead of them.

Walter Parks had built an empire, but he had done so on the blood of a former friend, and the sacrifice of his honor and his family and now his freedom. Sam shook his head in disgust, wondering how anyone could think even an empire was worth that extremely high price.

Parks looked like death, Sam couldn't help thinking as he studied the man sitting at the front of the courtroom. He must have aged twenty years in the past month. His hair had gone white, his skin gray, and there was a defeated stoop to his shoulders that contrasted distinctly with his former arrogantly assured posture. Was it possible the old man had acknowledged himself just how much he had thrown away in his long quest for wealth and power?

Sam turned his gaze to Jessica, who sat near the front of the courtroom between her brothers. Anna was in a different place, of course, secluded as were the other witnesses. Jessica was pale, but composed, listening attentively to Linda Carlton's testimony with no expression showing on her face.

It was torture to sit in the same room with her. Sam didn't even know why he was here, really. He'd simply felt he had to attend, in case Jessica needed him—most unlikely, considering she had her family to turn to now. Must be habit making him still watch out for her.

Damn, but she had hurt him with her lack of trust in him. How could she have believed he was still working with Walter even after all they had shared in Switzerland? And how could he have let himself care enough that she could break his heart that easily, he added with a low grunt of self-recrimination that made the tabloid reporter next to him glance at him in curiosity.

He ran into Jessica in a hallway very late that afternoon. She had just stepped out of the ladies' room, and he'd been returning from a walk outside to stretch his legs when they came face-to-face, their eyes locking.

Jessica's smile was a bit tremulous. "I saw you in the back of the courtroom earlier."

He nodded, keeping his hands in his pockets in case they attempted to reach for her despite his best intentions. "I wanted to know that you were going to be okay."

She moistened her lips with the tip of her tongue, and he was proud of himself that he didn't groan aloud. "I'll be fine, Sam. But thank you for being concerned."

He merely nodded.

She looked down to dig into the red tote bag she carried over one shoulder. "I brought something for you," she said.

He lifted an eyebrow. "How did you know I would be here?"

"I didn't, for certain." She pulled something from the bag and extended her hand.

His frown deepened when he found himself holding a set of what appeared to be car keys. "What is this?"

"The keys to my father's limo. I promised them to you if you helped me get to my mother, remember?"

Shaking his head, he held them out to her. "I don't want the damn limo."

But she had stepped back, putting her hands behind her. "I don't renege on my promises. I told my brothers what we said, and they agreed that I made a bargain. The limo will be delivered to you. You can sell it or drive it or whatever you want to do with it."

"Damn it, Jessica, that was meant as a joke. I didn't do anything for you in expectation of being paid."

"I know that now," she whispered. "It's taken me a while to realize that you were the only one who *wasn't* after anything from me. And I repaid you with such terrible accusations. I'm so sorry, Sam."

He could feel his heart opening again, slowly and painfully, still aching from the last time he'd let her in. There was a plea in her eyes when she gazed up at him, and he wanted very badly to give in to it, and to his own simmering need.

"Jessica. We're ready to go back in."

Somewhat impatiently, she looked beyond Sam, speaking to someone behind him. "I'll be right there, Cade." She looked back at Sam then. "Can you ever forgive me for doubting you?"

He leaned closer to her. Her mouth lifted to his when she realized his intention.

Ignoring the crowds milling around them, Sam kissed her slowly, lingeringly. And then he drew away. "Goodbye, Jessica. Be happy."

He dropped the limo keys into her tote bag before he turned and walked away, leaving a little part of his soul behind with her.

Chapter Fifteen

Jessica hung a delicate crystal ball from a fragrant fir branch, then stepped back to admire the way the faceted glass reflected the glow of the tiny lights woven into the tree. It was a lovely Christmas tree, she thought. Decorated in crystal ornaments and silver ribbons and hundreds of white lights, it sparkled cheerily in the big bow window of the mansion's front parlor.

She and Anna had considered not putting up a tree this year, but as the holiday rapidly approached, they reconsidered the decision. It would be Anna's first Christmas with her grandchildren, and she wanted them to have special memories of the occasion, though Noah was too young to remember, of course. Still, he would enjoy the lights and the presents, and his cousin, Stacy, would have a few memories of this holiday as she grew older. That seemed important to Anna.

It was important to Jessica, too. During the past difficult month she had been forcibly reminded of how much her family meant to her when they had all needed so badly to cling to each other.

Walter Parks was dead.

He had suffered a heart attack only hours after the end of the preliminary hearing, at which the judge had found more than sufficient evidence to hold him over for trial. There'd been little doubt in anyone's mind, including Walter's, that a trial would end in convictions on all the charges. Justice had caught up with him, and he had been unable to withstand the shock and humiliation.

No one could have known he was so ill, Jessica had tried to assure herself. It wasn't as if he'd told anyone he'd been suffering chest pains. They had simply assumed it was stress and mortification that had caused him to look so gray and sick at the hearing.

Still, she would always live with a pang of guilt that her last words to him had been such cold and angry ones. No matter what he had done, or for what reasons, he had been her father. She had loved him once, if for no other reason.

She and her siblings had grieved the loss of the father they had never really had, but the tragedy had brought them closer together. They had vowed not to take each other for granted so much in the future.

"It's beautiful, Jessica," Anna said as she came into the room holding a big basket of white poinsettias. "Stacy will say it looks like a fairy-tale tree."

"That's exactly what she'll say." Jessica turned away from the tree to smile at her mother, who was arranging the flowers on the mantel. "The house looks beautiful, Mother. Even prettier than it did when Dad brought in professional decorators every year to deck it out to impress the neighbors."

Anna had briefly considered selling the house after Walter's death, but she had decided to delay that decision for a while. Though her few years here had not been happy ones, this was where her children had been raised. It was a beautiful showcase of a house—all it had ever needed to make it a real home was love.

Anna stepped back to admire her handiwork. "I enjoyed decorating for Christmas when the twins were little. Then Walter decided that doing our own decorating was beneath our social status, and he insisted on bringing in professionals who paid little attention to what I wanted. Christmas changed after that."

Her face clouded for a moment, but then she shook her head. "We've agreed not to dwell on the unhappy memories. I promise I won't bring them up again."

"It's okay if you need to talk about it sometime," Jessica assured her gently. "I'm always here to listen."

"I know, darling, and I thank you. But there's really very little left to say about my unhappy past. I would rather concentrate on the future. It's going to be such a lovely Christmas, with everyone together once again."

Jessica smiled, nodded and tried to ignore the little pang in her heart at the thought of spending another holiday with her blissful newlywed siblings.

Anna seemed to have become quite perceptive about

Jessica's feelings during the past month together. She moved to sit beside her daughter on the couch that faced the tree. "What's wrong, darling? Are you sad about your father not being with you this Christmas? You needn't feel that you can't express that regret to me, you know, no matter how I might still feel about him."

"I'm sorry he couldn't have been the kind of father who would have appreciated the time together, but I've accepted his loss. I've even come to realize that it was better this way. Prison would have been torturous for him. Maybe he deserved to spend more time there, but I can't help being relieved that he didn't have to."

"You have such a kind heart." Anna lifted a hand to touch Jessica's cheek. "I should try to be more like you."

A little embarrassed, Jessica only smiled.

That smile faded fast when Anna dropped her hand and asked, "Have you heard from Sam since the hearing?"

Jessica kept her eyes focused intently on the tree. "Um, Sam? No, why do you ask?"

"You think I didn't recognize what I saw in your eyes when you looked at him? I've been in love a few times, you know. Enough to identify the emotion when I see it in my own daughter's face."

"I don't—" But Jessica stopped before she could complete the denial. She wouldn't start out her new relationship with her mother by lying to her.

"I did fall in love with him," she admitted quietly. "But even if he had started to love me in return—which is a big if, since he was hurt very badly in a divorce and wasn't eager to get involved that seriously again—I blew it by not trusting him when I should have. I hurt him, Mother, when all he was trying to do was help me. He can't forgive me for that."

Anna took her hand, cradling it in both of hers. "Have you asked him to forgive you?"

"Yes." She remembered the way he had kissed her in the courthouse before he had walked away from her. There had been no mistaking that it was a kiss of goodbye.

Whatever chance she might have had of making Sam love her had died that night in his car when she had accused him of calling her father to have her kidnapped from the airport.

"It wasn't just my lack of trust in him," she added with a sad shake of her head. "He sat through the entire hearing, you know. He heard exactly what kind of man my father was. Between that and all the other emotional baggage our family carries, who could blame him for wanting to run?"

Anna seemed to take offense at that. "I don't see those old scandals deterring Sara from loving Cade."

"Of course not. Her family's part of it all."

"And what about Louanne? She has willingly brought her son into our family to live as one of us."

"By the time Noah's old enough to understand, this will all be ancient history as far as he's concerned."

"And Lazhar? How do you explain his continuing loyalty to Emily?"

"He's the king of a country very far away from this one. He certainly doesn't have to worry about salacious San Francisco gossip."

"And you think Sam *does* worry about that sort of thing?"

Jessica cleared her throat. "He has his business reputation to consider."

"Ah. Perhaps my impression of him was wrong. I thought he was a man who cared little about what other people thought of him—except for you, of course. A man to whom money wasn't particularly important."

"You don't understand, Mother."

Anna gave her a sad smile. "I have so many regrets about my life, my darling. So very many. But the one thing that hurts me most, and will always hurt me, is that I didn't fight harder to stay with the ones I loved. I was too afraid to take the risk."

"Look, it doesn't really matter why he walked away. The simple truth is that he didn't want me." Jessica choked a little then. "He didn't want me."

"Then he's an idiot," Anna said promptly, reaching out to take Jessica in her arms. "Any man who wouldn't want you is an idiot."

For the first time in her life, Jessica was able to cry on her mother's shoulder. Yet not even the comfort she found there completely eased the pain.

Sam called himself an idiot even as he approached the front door of the mansion. A huge wreath hung in the center of that door. Other decorations gave a cheerful holiday air to the formerly cold and formal-looking house. A huge Christmas tree was visible in one of the front windows, looking as if it was ready for a happy family to gather beneath it with their gifts.

Several cars parked in the circular driveway indicated that members of the family had gathered for this

Christmas Eve. Though darkness had already fallen, the front gates stood invitingly open, which had allowed Sam to drive through without difficulty. The security consultant in him cringed at the carelessness, but he couldn't help thinking of how much more welcoming the Parks estate seemed now than it had the first time he had seen it.

He stood for quite a while in front of that door, trying to decide whether to ring the bell or simply turn around and go. He could leave the prettily wrapped package he held on the doorstep. It had Jessica's name written on a little card, and even though he hadn't signed his name, she would know who had left the gift.

If she wanted to call him afterward, she knew how to reach him. If she didn't call...well, that would be a message in itself.

Because he could so easily imagine himself following through with that plan, and because it made him feel like a coward just to consider it, he made himself reach out and ring the bell. If he was lucky, a member of the housekeeping staff would answer and he could leave the gift with her. That way he wouldn't interrupt Jessica's holiday with her family, he rationalized.

He probably looked like a delivery guy in his battered brown leather jacket, oatmeal-colored pullover and old, faded jeans. Maybe he should have dressed up a little more, but he'd left his house on impulse and hadn't stopped to...

Of all the people there must be in that monstrously big house, it had to be Jessica who answered the door.

Sam figured he should have expected it, considering the way things had unfolded between them so far.

She looked stunned to see him. There was no other word to describe the look on her face when she recognized him. "Sam!"

"The, um, gates were open," he said, motioning vaguely behind him. "I hope it's okay that I just drove on in."

"Of course. We're expecting Derek and Benton to stop in this evening for a Christmas Eve visit with Mother. That's why the gates are… Why are you here?"

Damned if he could remember at the moment. Not when she was standing so close, looking so pretty in her snug red sweater and dark, low-riding jeans that showed just a sliver of flat tummy. Heeled boots gave an illusion of height, and silver hoops swung from her ears. She had cut her hair, he noted automatically. Still shoulder length, it was more layered now, a little shaggier. He liked it.

"Sam?"

"Yeah." She smelled like Christmas, he thought. Sort of a mixture of evergreen and gingerbread, hinting that she had been decorating and baking. A delicious combination. He blinked and held out the package he'd been holding. "I brought you a present."

He doubted she could have looked more wary if he'd said, "I brought you a box full of poisonous snakes." She looked at the box as if she expected it to explode. "A present?"

"Yeah. Look, maybe this was a bad idea. I didn't mean to interrupt your time with your family." He thrust the package at her and started to turn away.

"Sam, wait. Please don't go."

He froze in response to the note of pleading in her voice. She gave him a shy smile when he turned back to look at her again. "You aren't interrupting anything."

He swallowed and nodded.

"May I open this now?"

"Sure. If you want to."

She closed the front door behind her, giving them privacy in the cool night air. Little bells jingled merrily in the wreath with the motion. Stripping away the wrapping paper, she handed it to him to hold while she opened the box inside.

A moment later she looked back up at him, and this time there were tears streaming down her cheeks. "This is…perfect," she whispered.

Feeling incredibly awkward, he resisted an impulse to shuffle his feet. "It's just— It isn't— I just thought you might like it."

"I love it." The gift was a high quality snow globe, the thick glass orb supported by a wooden base. Inside the globe was a snowy landscape featuring an intricately detailed Swiss chalet with the Alps in the background. Jessica shook the globe lightly, making snow swirl around the scene. "It reminds me of that morning…."

"'Breakfast in a snow globe,'" he quoted her, knowing exactly which morning she referred to. "That's what it made me think of, too."

The expression in her eyes almost made his heart stop. "I came here thinking maybe I would ask if you would like to see me again sometime," he said roughly. "Have dinner, maybe, or see a movie. But now—"

"You've changed your mind?"

"Yeah. I don't want to date you, Jessica. My feelings for you are way beyond that. I know I'm not part of your social stratum—hell, I'm blue collar to my roots—and I know I'm too old for you, and I know I'm not the easiest guy in the world to get along with at times. If you need more time for me to convince you that we belong together, I'll try to be patient and court you the way you deserve to be courted. Just don't tell me there isn't a chance for us. Don't—"

"I love you, Sam."

The quiet interruption made his words jam in his throat. "You—"

"I don't care about any of those things you see as obstacles between us. I've loved you since our first dance in Zurich. I thought I had thrown it all away when I lashed out at you after seeing my father that night. I never thought of you as just a way to get back at my father, but I can see where you must have believed that when I behaved so unfairly toward you. I thought I'd hurt you too badly for you to ever forgive me."

"I thought you had, too," Sam admitted, regretting the pain he saw in her eyes in response to the admission. "I told myself it wasn't worth setting myself up to be hurt like that again. And that you were better off without me, anyway. But I couldn't stay away. You're all I can think about, all I care about. I need you back in my life."

Holding the snow globe in both hands, she moved closer to him and lifted her face toward his. He took her in his arms and crushed her mouth beneath his, neither noticing nor caring that the globe was digging into his chest.

* * *

Sam slid the red sweater over Jessica's head and tossed it carelessly to one side of the bedroom in her cottage. "Red underwear," he murmured with a smile, stroking her nipple through her lacy bra. "Have I ever mentioned that I really go for red underwear?"

"No, as a matter of fact—" His mouth covered hers, smothering her reply.

After he had kissed her until her head was spinning, he eased off her jeans, finding and approving of the tiny red panties beneath. He took his time removing the undergarments, kissing and caressing and teasing every inch of her until she was the one who started frantically stripping them away, longing desperately for the feel of his bare skin against hers.

And when there was nothing left between them but desire, she pushed him onto his back and proceeded to drive him as crazy with need as he had her. She might be rather new at this sort of thing, she thought as a groan tore from his throat, but she was a very fast learner.

He caught her hips in his hands, guiding her to him as she straddled him. She lowered her mouth to his, letting their tongues mate even as he thrust upward to join them. Switzerland hadn't been paradise, after all, Jessica mused with her last coherent thought. Paradise had turned out to be right here, in her very own home.

"I'm not sure I've told you that I love you."

Jessica smiled and stroked a finger down the center of Sam's chest, which was still rising and falling rather rapidly. "Oh, I think you've made it clear enough."

"I'll say it, anyway. I love you, Jessica."

She kissed his shoulder. "I love you, too."

Resting his cheek against her hair, he sighed deeply. Contentedly.

After several long, silent moments, he spoke again. "I'm sorry about your father."

She nestled more snugly into him. "I got your flowers. Thank you."

The card had said simply, "I'm sorry for your loss. Sam." She had wondered at the time what he would have thought if he'd known she was hurting as badly over losing him as she had been the father who'd been so estranged from her.

"I hope you know that he did love you, in his own warped way. He really did want me to keep you safe, even as he worked to stop you from having what you wanted so badly."

"I know. He just wasn't capable of loving his family more than he loved his power."

She told him then about Caroline, and the way Walter had used and twisted their friendship with his money and his lies. About the fear she had lived with that she was losing her mind.

"My God, I'm sorry, Jessica. So many people you cared about have hurt you and betrayed you. No wonder it's so hard for you to trust anyone now."

She lifted her head then to look at him. "I trust you with my life. And with all my heart. I never want you to doubt that again. Of all the good people I've known, you are the most honorable, Sam."

She watched in fascination as a flush worked its way

up from his throat to his cheeks. "Don't make me out
to be some sort of hero," he said gruffly. "I'll only end
up disappointing you if you do that. I'm a long way from
perfect. I've got plenty of flaws."

"I've come to realize that everyone has flaws. It's
what we accomplish despite them that matters. I don't
expect you to be perfect, Sam. I know you'll hurt my
feelings at times, and you'll make me furious at others.
Just as I can guarantee that I'll do things to make you
mad, since I seem to have a talent for that. But the one
thing I believe implicitly is that you will never disap-
point me."

"I promise that I will never intentionally betray your
trust in me," he said a bit shakily. "I will love you and
stand by you for the rest of my life, if you'll have me."

Her throat tightened. "Careful, Sam. That sounds a
lot like a proposal. And I know how you feel about getting married again."

"No, you don't. I want nothing more than to marry
you, Jessica Parks. I want a real marriage this time,
based on love and trust and total commitment. I can
learn to trust again if you can."

Her eyes had filled with pesky tears again, but her
voice was steady. "I'll never betray your trust in me, either. You have my word on that—and I would die before I break that promise."

He stroked his fingertips along the line of her jaw.
"What have I done to deserve you?"

"I'm the one who should be asking that. Why don't
we just agree to spend the rest of our lives making the
best of our good fortune?"

"Is that a yes?"

She smiled against his lips. "That is most definitely a yes."

She knew her family would be wondering what was keeping her away from them for so long, even though she had left word that she would be in her cottage. She knew they would be eager to meet Sam and would be delighted to hear about her engagement—especially Anna, who had decided that she approved of Sam when he had been so kind to her at the airport. But there was really no hurry, she decided as Sam twisted to slide her beneath him. They had the rest of their lives to let love heal the wounds of the past.

As she wrapped her arms around Sam's neck, she realized that there was no more powerful cure.

* * * * *

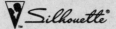

SPECIAL EDITION™

This January 2005...don't miss
the next book in bestselling author

Victoria Pade's

brand-new miniseries...

Northbridge
Nuptials

Where a walk down the aisle is never far behind.

HAVING THE
BACHELOR'S BABY
(SE #1658)

After sharing one incredible night in the arms of
Ben Walker, Clair Cabot is convinced she'll never
see the sexy reformed bad boy again. Then fate
throws her for a loop when she's forced to deal
with Ben in a professional capacity. Should she
also confess the very personal secret that's
growing in her belly?

Available at your favorite retail outlet.

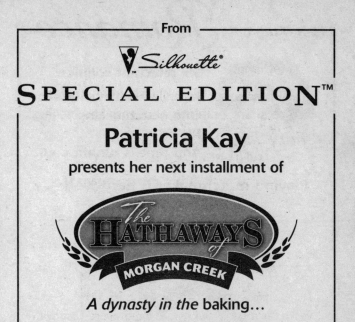

If you enjoyed what you just read,
then we've got an offer you can't resist!

Take 2 bestselling
love stories FREE!

Plus get a FREE surprise gift!

Clip this page and mail it to Silhouette Reader Service™

IN U.S.A.	IN CANADA
3010 Walden Ave.	P.O. Box 609
P.O. Box 1867	Fort Erie, Ontario
Buffalo, N.Y. 14240-1867	L2A 5X3

YES! Please send me 2 free Silhouette Special Edition® novels and my free surprise gift. After receiving them, if I don't wish to receive anymore, I can return the shipping statement marked cancel. If I don't cancel, I will receive 6 brand-new novels every month, before they're available in stores! In the U.S.A., bill me at the bargain price of $4.24 plus 25¢ shipping and handling per book and applicable sales tax, if any*. In Canada, bill me at the bargain price of $4.99 plus 25¢ shipping and handling per book and applicable taxes**. That's the complete price and a savings of at least 10% off the cover prices—what a great deal! I understand that accepting the 2 free books and gift places me under no obligation ever to buy any books. I can always return a shipment and cancel at any time. Even if I never buy another book from Silhouette, the 2 free books and gift are mine to keep forever.

235 SDN DZ9D
335 SDN DZ9E

Name	(PLEASE PRINT)	
Address	Apt.#	
City	State/Prov.	Zip/Postal Code

Not valid to current Silhouette Special Edition® subscribers.

Want to try two free books from another series?
Call 1-800-873-8635 or visit www.morefreebooks.com.

* Terms and prices subject to change without notice. Sales tax applicable in N.Y.
** Canadian residents will be charged applicable provincial taxes and GST.
All orders subject to approval. Offer limited to one per household.
® are registered trademarks owned and used by the trademark owner and or its licensee.

SPED04R   ©2004 Harlequin Enterprises Limited